8/06

Once again, to every reader who opens the cover
and turns the pages, thank you

For information address Hyperion Books for Children, 114 Fifth Avenue, New
York, New York 10011-5690.
First Edition
1 3 5 7 9 10 8 6 4 2
This book is set in 11-point Goudy.
Printed in the United States of America
Reinforced binding
Library of Congress Cataloging-in-Publication Data on file.
ISBN 0-7868-3690-3 (tr. ed.)
Visit www.jumpatthesun.com

D0961806

PLAYED

DANA DAVIDSON

Jump at the Sun

*H*yperion
NEW YORK

Chapter 1

"This party is played, man," Ian Striver complained to his boy Michael.

"Oh, baby!" Michael yelled. He scanned the Cross cafeteria, now decked in strobe lighting, spinning reflective balls that hung from the ceiling, and dim blue lights.

"Damn, you're already blowed!" Ian said.

"Hell, yeah. I wouldn't come to one of these things any other way."

"You're sick, fool, sick."

"Well, let me tell you, I'm gettin' better all the time," Michael said.

Ian just shook his head and looked around the winter dance. This was the party that Cross High School threw each

1

December. Students crowded the floor, dancing to the beat, while teachers patrolled and talked to one another on the sidelines. Ian and his crew had shown up as a joke, really. After stepping through here they were planning to hang out at the Cradle, a dance club for teens, off East Jefferson Avenue. "Why are we here, Mike?" Ian asked.

"I don't know, man. Just relax. Check out the honeys. We might see something good."

"Ain't nothing much up in here, man. All these young things. Too easy."

"Easy, huh?"

"As one and one," Ian said.

Several girls came over to where Ian and his boys stood. "What's up?" the shortest one asked Dante.

"You, girl," he answered, looking her up and down slowly.

"Yeah, right," she answered, her tone sexy, "that's why I never got your call, huh?"

"I'm gonna call you, for real," he said. "A brother's just been busy, you know. But I'm about to ring you."

"You'd better," she said. She leaned over and whispered something in his ear, and all the guys watched as Dante slipped his hand to her waist, then her hip.

When she pulled away, he released her and smiled. "Bet," he told her, "you got me curious now."

"That's how I want you," she said. Then she and her girls turned and walked away.

The guys watched them melt into the crowd. Then Dante turned to Ian and said, "But can you do it like that, young pledge?"

"That was good, I have to admit," Ian said. "But I think I can at *least* match that."

"I guess you think you're the original player, huh?" Michael said.

"I didn't say all that, but since you said it . . ." Ian chuckled. His eyes roved over the dance floor, lingering for a few moments on a girl near him who danced fast and nasty. She saw him looking, and they held each other's eyes for several seconds. She was just the kind of girl he liked, pretty and dressed to impress, with a little bit of snob thrown in to make her a challenge.

"Well, man," Michael said. "If you're all that, prove it."

"I don't have to prove it to you or anybody else. I've never had a problem gettin' a shorty to give some of that up." Ian flicked his eyes over the dancing girl once more before he looked back at Michael.

"Yeah, I don't know why all those girls like your ugly butt, anyway," Michael laughed.

Ian's hazel eyes flashed as he lifted his finely chiseled chin. "Don't hate, man, you know I'm pretty," Ian joked.

"Whatever. I'll hit you with fifty bills, though, if you prove it," Michael said.

Ian looked at Michael closely to see if he was serious. "Serious?"

"As a fat man's heart attack."

"What do I have to do?"

"What do you think? What do players do?"

"I just want you to make it clear. I don't want you

backing out later, saying you can't give me my money 'cause that ain't what you meant."

Michael laughed because it was true, he would try to pull some mess like that. "You ain't right, man."

"Whatever."

"You gotta get a little nobody to give up the nasty."

Ian felt some nervous excitement, but he just nodded his head as though what his boy said didn't touch him. "Okay."

"Bet. But I get to pick her."

"Naw, fool!"

"Hell, yeah. It's my money at stake."

"And my thang." They both laughed. "Don't pick a flat-out dog, Mike, man."

"All right. But she's gotta have a little puppy chow in the mix, or it won't be any fun for me."

"And she's gotta be clean, Mike."

"Hell, yes!" They gave each other plays. "I'm gonna pick her for you, Ian."

Ian rubbed his palms discreetly on his oversized designer jeans and Michael began prowling the dimly lit cafeteria. He'd point at a girl who was totally out of the question, and he and the other FBI guys would fall out laughing as Ian violently waved him on. Finally Michael came up on a group of girls who were all standing together, wearing tight jeans and even tighter tops. Ian evaluated the group. They looked young, like ninth or tenth graders. There were a couple of cuties. One had short hair, light skin, and a shapely body. Another was tall with long hair, chocolate skin, slanted eyes, a tiny waist, and a big butt. Pick one of those, Ian thought.

The third girl had brown skin, narrow hips, small breasts, and medium-length hair with way too much gel holding it into a tired, hard ponytail. Her jeans and T-shirt were so tight that they didn't look seductive; they looked painful. Ian groaned. She's the one, he thought. To confirm his fears Michael pointed her out for him and nodded his head.

"It's all yours, player," Michael said when he came back over.

"Damn, man."

"I know," Michael said laughing. "But, it shouldn't be hard for a player like you to squeeze up on that."

"God, she doesn't look like she's ever kissed anyone, much less had sex."

"What, Ian, are you scared to tap a virgin?" Tamar asked.

"Please, a virgin would only make it sweeter," Ian said, eyeing the girl across the floor. "How long do I have?" he asked Michael.

"For you? You're kinda young, so I'll extend the normal time." The boys grinned at one another. "Three weeks."

"Three weeks!"

"I'll tell you what," Michael said, really getting into it. "A real player could do more than get in the panties, he could make her fall for him. I'll give you a hundred dollars if you get her to give it up *and* fall for you."

"In three weeks?"

"Three weeks. We'll make this your third and final challenge," Mike added. "You get us the proof that you completed it and you will definitely be at the Freak Fest a month from now." Ian's heartbeat picked up and a smile crept onto his face. The only way for him to get to the Freak Fest was to be an FBI member. Ian was popular, but he wouldn't be one of the few guys invited to that party of about 100 kids if he wasn't FBI. The invitations only went to about thirty-five guys from Cross: top jocks and the *extremely* popular. The rest of the guests would be some of the finest and freakiest girls Ian had ever dreamed of. This year the Freak Fest would be at Michael's parents' lavish six-bedroom mansion.

Ian looked across the dance floor at the girl again. Damn, he thought, I don't even know her name. Plus, as he looked at her, he realized that he felt absolutely no attraction. For a moment he thought he should just get out of this stupid bet. But he knew he wouldn't.

Ian had just made it into the induction phase of FBI, Freaky Boys Incorporated, in October. It was an exclusive underground fraternal group at Cross composed of juniors and seniors. Ever since ninth grade Ian had longed to be in FBI. They were some of the best-dressed, best-looking, and most popular guys in school. The catch was, you *had* to fit in. Too much thinking for yourself, and as far as the FBI was concerned, you could be by your own damn self. Michael was a senior and second in command. His dares were pretty much tests. Meet 'em or get to steppin'.

"Quit stallin', Ian. Make your move."

Ian sighed and moved away. Mike was right. It was time to do this. But he wasn't enjoying it. It wasn't the first time he'd wondered why he did some of the stuff he did to be in FBI.

Still, he *had* gotten picked by the best crowd, and now,

he was nearly in. He didn't want to jeopardize that by acting like he didn't want to hurt some girl's feeling. And this wasn't the worst thing that he could do. It wasn't drugs, it wasn't stealing or something like that. It was sex. Hell, that couldn't be all bad. Not at all, Ian reasoned.

Ian circled the dance floor and stopped behind the trio of girls. He leaned over and spoke into the plain girl's ear. "You wanna dance?" She turned around and peered at Ian in the dim lighting. Ian's small hope that she might be cuter up close fell flat.

"Yeah, sure," she said.

Ian led her out onto the dance floor and fell into his dance steps. He stood fairly close to her, feeling her out, seeing how she reacted. She didn't move away from him so he moved in a little closer. Even if the party was weak, the music was tight, and Ian noted that the girl did know how to move. Ian's next steps brought him in up close to her, and he allowed the rhythm of his dancing to cause him to bump and grind against her. She extended her arms above her head, moved to his rhythm for a few moments, and then discreetly moved away. Ian smiled to himself. He could respect that. He figured that if she let him grind up on her it would be that much easier to get her to give it up. He didn't try to press up on her again. Instead he kept it close, but not too close.

When the song ended Ian led her away from her friends, over to a less crowded part of the cafeteria. He looked over in Michael's direction and found him watching. Michael smiled when Ian caught his eye. Ian nodded, then turned to the girl.

"What's your name?" Ian yelled above the pounding music.

"What?" she yelled back.

"What's your name?"

"I can't hear you!" she said.

"Come on," Ian said, and led her out into the hallway where it was well lit and a lot quieter. As they stood in the hall Ian looked her over more carefully. She wasn't bad, really, he thought. But he preferred them *fine*. He noted that her hair and clothes were messed up, her body wasn't inspirational, and her face wasn't even that interesting. But her eyes were nice. They were black, black, black. They absorbed light like velvet, flat, deep, and luxurious. "What's up?" Ian asked.

"Nothing."

"What's your name?"

"Kylie."

"I'm Ian."

"I know."

"You know, huh?"

"Yes."

"How do you know my name?" Ian asked, fishing for a compliment.

Kylie wasn't helping out. "I don't know."

"Well, I just wanted to ask you if I could have your number."

She looked at Ian for a moment, studying him mildly. Then she said, "Sure, okay."

Ian didn't know what to make of her less-than-enthusiastic

attitude. He got the number anyway though, and walked her back into the dance.

"Was that so bad?" Michael asked when Ian returned. The other guys laughed and gave each other plays.

"Whatever, man," Ian said. He was taking one last look around the dance. "Let's bounce."

"All right," Michael said, and they all left.

Dez and Tracy had been watching when Kylie and Ian came back into the dance. When Kylie came to stand next to them again they were about ready to burst.

"What's up, girl?" Dez asked.

"What?" Kylie said stalling.

"Don't 'what' me, Kylie. What's up with this Ian thing?" Dez asked.

"I don't know. There is no 'Ian thing,'" Kylie said. "He asked me to dance. Then he asked me for my number."

"What's this about?" Dez now directed her question to Tracy as though Tracy might prove a better source of information.

"I don't know. Have you two been talking or something?" Tracy asked.

"No." Kylie watched as Ian and the other guys left the dance. "We've never said a word to each other."

"I guess you caught his eye," Dez said.

"I guess," Kylie said thoughtfully. "I guess."

Chapter 2

Kylie had a feeling that something would happen to her when she got up on the morning of the winter dance. She didn't know what. She wasn't even sure that the something would be something good. When she woke that morning and looked at her reflection in the mirror she seemed to see more than her medium brown skin, her round face, thin lips, and deep black eyes. There was more than her disobedient hair and her thin frame.

All day at school she had gone about her normal routine. But there just behind everything was this odd anticipation. After school she'd gone home and done what she always did: take care of her younger sister and brother. She helped them with their homework, put on dinner, straightened up around the house, and tried to get some of her own homework done.

When she'd finished all of that, Kylie was tired, but looking forward to the dance. So she showered, which made her feel better, and then got dressed. She didn't have much to choose from, wardrobe-wise, but she thought that she looked all right in a bright pink T-shirt and her only new pants this school year: dark blue jeans. Her hair would have to stay in the same ponytail that it had been in all week, secured into place by gel, the nightly application of a hair wrap, and sheer will. Kylie thought of herself as plain, but she liked her hair least of all. The problem was that she didn't have the money to take better care of it.

Her mother came home before 9 P.M., just as Kylie finished getting herself ready.

"So you're goin' out, huh?" Kylie's mother asked. Jillian was slim, like her daughter, and their faces were nearly mirror reflections.

"Yes," Kylie said. "Renee and Stevie have already eaten and done their homework. I put your plate in the refrigerator."

"You goin' with Desiree and Tracy?"

"Yes."

"All right," Jillian said. "Be back here by twelve-thirty, okay?"

"Yes, Mama."

Jillian nodded. The doorbell rang and Kylie snatched up her coat as she headed to answer the door. A few seconds later, she rounded the corner with her two friends behind her.

"Hi, Jillian," Tracy and Desiree said together.

"Hey," Jillian answered.

"I'm gone," Kylie yelled up the stairs to her little sister and brother. The two children came crashing downstairs, calling, "hey Mama" as they hugged their mom, then Kylie.

"When are you comin' back?" Renee wanted to know.

"Late, Nae Nae," Kylie said. "You'll be asleep when I come home."

"Are you takin' us to the library to see the puppet show tomorrow?" Stevie wanted to know.

"I told you I was," Kylie added affectionately. "Now, go ahead and finish the story. Go give Mama a kiss, then let her be, she's tired.

"I'll see you later," Kylie added. "Bye, Mama."

Kylie headed out the door with her friends. "Girl, it's like you're their real mama," Tracy commented once they were outside.

"Straight up, Kylie. You do everything for them but pay the bills," Dez said.

Kylie smiled softly. "I know, but I'm not their mama. I'm their sister. And I'm ready to go out and have a little fun."

"You don't get to have enough fun, Kylie," Tracy said.

"True, but don't remind me."

"I don't know how good this winter dance is supposed to be," Dez said.

"Yeah, it might be pretty lame," Tracy said.

Kylie shrugged. "Maybe, but I just want to go somewhere. We can go to The Biz if it's boring. As long as I'm back home by twelve-thirty I'm all right."

Kylie got in the warm, dark cocoon of Desiree's car and breathed deeply. *What is it?* she wondered. For the feeling that something was going to happen still had not gone away. It had stayed after she had given a correct answer in English class about a short story she barely understood. It had lingered after she got her Algebra III quiz back and found an A- on the top of her paper. She was struggling so badly in Algebra III that she would celebrate, absolutely celebrate, if she squeaked by with a C. And when Terrance Wells, a cute boy in her math class, had said that he wanted to be sure to get a dance with her tonight, it had still remained.

But when Ian Striver began to make his way around the dance floor, Kylie just knew that he was headed to her. When he leaned over and asked her to dance, that feeling of expectancy began to dissipate, and by the time she had recited her telephone number for him, it had entirely disappeared.

Chapter 3

"Ian! Ian!"

Ian rolled his eyes as his mother screamed his name from downstairs. "What, Ma?"

"Come here, boy!"

Ian dragged himself down the stairs to the kitchen and stood before his mother. She was angry and fed up, her fists rammed into her hips.

"Ian, what is wrong with you?"

"What?"

"Little boy, if you 'what' me again, I'll knock you on your tail."

"I'm gonna clean the kitchen, Ma."

"Gonna clean it? Boy, it's twelve-thirty in the afternoon.

You were out all night. I let you go to that dance at school and Lord knows where you were until one-thirty in the morning. Now you stand in my face telling me you gonna get to what I told you to do last night?"

Ian just stood there looking at her. She didn't really want a response. She wanted to vent. He stifled a sigh and waited her out.

"Now, I told you before you left last night that I wanted this kitchen cleaned up this morning. And that's what I meant, Ian. If you don't have this kitchen spick-and-span in a hurry, your behind won't be going anywhere for the next two weeks."

"All right, Madame Mama," Ian said. He reached out to tickle her.

"Stop it, fool!" she said slapping at his hand while biting back a smile.

"I'm so sorry, Madame Mama, I don't know what got into me. I know it's late in the day and you handed down your commandments yesterday, and I'm so sorry, Madame Mama."

"Get started," she said, fully smiling now. Then she hit him lightly one more time on the shoulder.

She left Ian alone in the kitchen, and he started sorting out the mess. It wasn't that he really minded doing his chores, but as far as he was concerned, there was always something better to do. If he could get away with putting his work off, he would.

Ms. Striver earned a good salary working the afternoon shift at Ford Motor Company. Her job and Mr. Striver's financial support kept Ian and his older sister Kim well taken care of. Ms. Striver did expect her children to do their share, though. They prepared their own meals and Kim did the grocery shopping. Ms. Striver also had them do most of the housework. Just because they were doing all right didn't mean she would raise spoiled kids.

They lived in a small house on the southeast side of Detroit. It wasn't fancy, but it was very comfortable. Ian had his own room with his own music system, television, and DVD player. The neighborhood was nothing to brag about, but if you minded your own business you didn't have to worry much.

Ian's parents had been divorced for five years. His father had gotten remarried two years ago and his new wife was pregnant with their second child. Although Mr. Striver kept up his financial end, Ian and Kim rarely saw him. His father worked a lot, was busy with his new family, and didn't have a lot of time for Ian and Kim. They were the second-place family now, and it hurt.

When Ian finished the kitchen he went ahead and did the rest of his chores. It was better to keep his mama off his back. While cleaning his room he noticed the jeans he had worn last night tossed on a chair. He picked them up and emptied the pockets. There was that girl Kylie's telephone number. He read it over, pictured her, and felt nothing. Then he did feel something: exasperation. Not with her, but with the situation. It seemed like a waste of time to push up on a girl he didn't even like. Ian sighed, went into the hallway, got the telephone off the stand, and brought it into his room. He dialed and waited.

"Hello?"

"Hello, may I speak to Kylie?"

"This is she."

"What's up, Kylie? It's Ian."

"Oh, hey, Ian. What's going on"

"Nothing much. Did you like the party?"

"It was okay."

"Yeah. So, what grade are you in?" Ian checked the clock on his wall. Ten minutes. He'd put in ten minutes of this and then he was off. Ian couldn't care less about this Kylie, and he didn't feel motivated to hold a conversation with her.

"I'm in the eleventh," she answered. With over 2,500 students at Cross High, it wasn't hard to go for three years and not know someone at the Detroit school.

"You are? I thought you were in the tenth."

"Really? Why?"

"You look younger. I'm in the eleventh, too."

"I know."

"Let's see, last night you already knew my name, now I see you know my grade too. What else do you know about me?"

"You hang out in the hallway on three between classes and after school."

"How do you know so much about me?"

"I hear things. Anyway, you kind of stick out."

"Do I, now?" Ian smiled.

"Just a tiny bit," Kylie said.

"I'm sort of flattered."

"You would be."

"What does that mean?" Ian had caught the sarcasm in her voice. "You think I'm conceited, don't you?"

"I don't know. Are you?"

"You're a trip. No, I'm not conceited." She was turning out to be something a little unexpected.

"Come on now, not even a little?" Kylie teased. With his even, chestnut brown skin, sculptured features, full lips, 5'10" slim but muscular build, and hazel eyes, Kylie figured he could afford to be a little conceited.

Ian laughed out loud. "All right, if you don't tell anybody, I'll admit it, I'm a tiny bit conceited. Does that make me bad?" he asked.

"No, not especially. I have a feeling that there are some other things that might make you bad, though."

"Is that right?"

"You tell me."

"You're a little right." Ian admitted, laughing again. They talked for a while, the conversation weaving easily between the mundane and the eventful. Ian said, "So where did you get a name like Kylie?"

"My name is really Kyle. I'm named for my grandfather. He died of a heart attack the night of the day that I was born. So we were here on Earth at the same time for only a few hours."

"Oh man, that's messed up."

"Yeah. My mama was crazy about her dad. So she named me after him."

"That's all right," Ian said appreciatively. "Do you mind having a man's name, though?"

"Oh, it's cool. Everyone's told me about him, and he

sounds like he was a good man. People tell me that my Uncle Jonathon is just like him, and I love my Uncle Jonathon to death. Mostly people call me Kylie."

"Kylie. Yeah, that sounds more feminine. So how long did you stay at the dance last night?"

"Until about eleven. Longer than you."

"Like you said, it was just okay."

"It was. But I don't get out that much, so . . ."

"Are your parents really strict or something?"

"No, not really. But it just works out where I don't get out a lot," Kylie said.

"Who do you live with?" Ian checked his clock again. More than half an hour had passed and he no longer cared.

"My mama, little sister, and little brother."

"You're the big sis, then."

"Yep. Who do you live with?" she asked.

"I live with my sister Kim—she's twenty—and my mama."

"So you're the baby, huh?"

"Yeah."

"Where's your father?" Kylie asked.

"My parents are divorced. He remarried a couple of years ago, and now they have one kid and another one on the way. What about yours?"

"My mama and daddy were never married. He doesn't have any other children."

"Do you see him a lot?"

"No." The absence of her father was a sore spot that she didn't feel like getting into.

19

"I don't see mine that much either. I used to see him more before he got married again."

"That's messed up."

"Yeah . . . Anyway, what curriculum are you in?" Cross High School was a school of choice where students were admitted by examination and application. It was big, with six floors and about 2,500 students, all divided into ten different curriculums that students had to pursue, in the same way college students pursued their majors. It was well known nationally for producing high-achieving graduates in every field.

"Business. What about you?"

"Architecture."

"Yeah?"

"Yeah," Ian said. "Why do you say it like that?"

"I'm just a little surprised. I didn't really figure you for architecture, maybe performing arts or something like that."

"Well, I do sing. I do some acting, too."

"You sing, huh? Any good?" She'd heard him sing, but she wanted to see what he'd say.

"Some people say so," Ian said modestly.

"I'd like to hear you sometime."

"I'd like that, too." Ian checked the clock again. They'd been talking for nearly an hour. He was having a good time, but he still had his three-week deadline to meet. "I was wondering if you wanted to hook up on Tuesday. Maybe we could take a drive or go to laser tag or something?"

Kylie paused and thought a moment. "I'll tell you what. Let me see if I can and you call me back later so that I can let you know, okay?"

"Yeah, that sounds good." They said good-bye and hung up.

Ian sat for a moment thinking it all over. Three weeks to get this girl to sleep with him and fall for him. He wasn't really *that* conceited. He knew it would be a challenge. Plus, now she wasn't this somebody he didn't know. She had a name, a personality, a voice. She had made him laugh and got him interested.

Ian shook his head. After this he wouldn't have to take any more challenges from Michael or anyone else in FBI. He would be glad when this was over.

Chapter 4

Kylie hung up the telephone and drew her knees up under her chin. *Ian Striver. Called me. Ian Striver called me.* And they were probably going to go out. Why, though? Kylie wondered. She didn't kid herself. She didn't think she was that good-looking and she knew she wasn't popular. Ian, on the other hand, was so fine and popular that he could have any girl he wanted. Kylie wasn't sure what, but she felt that something wasn't quite right.

But the truth was that she wanted something more to happen to her. She went to school, took care of her siblings, kept their house clean, did homework, and saw her girlfriends from time to time. But that wasn't enough. It seemed to Kylie that a perfectly healthy, reasonably intelligent teenage girl ought to be able to get into more than that. Kylie felt as if her life was more like that of a thirty-five-year-old than a sixteen-year-old. So while she had her suspicions about why Ian was taking time with her, she was going to let it ride and see where it took her.

Even if her life wasn't perfect, she was glad that she had her two best friends. Kylie had known Desiree and Tracy since the sixth grade and they talked about nearly everything. Kylie was very connected to them, but at the same time she always felt just a little bit behind them.

Then her thoughts turned back to Ian.

Ian Striver. Kylie smiled to herself. Kylie had first noticed Ian in a talent show two years ago when they were ninth graders. He performed with a group of four other good-looking boys. They'd sung a romantic ballad, each singing nearly equal parts. When Ian had his solo he'd stepped to the microphone with bravado, but Kylie had sensed his nervous excitement. He had been good, and the crowd in the auditorium had responded wildly. Maybe, just a little, she had a crush on Ian after that. A tiny, hidden, rarely thought of crush.

But it was never a serious crush because there was no way that Ian would be interested in her, or so she thought.

Today on the phone it felt like they'd connected. The memory of his voice in her ears made her insides hum. The day seemed to lift and sing before her, full of new and unexpected pleasures.

Kylie got up and started dinner. It would be a simple meal: chicken soup from scratch, biscuits from the can, and a

23

salad. She daydreamed about Ian as she prepared the food. By the time she had the soup simmering and the salad tossed she heard her mother's key in the door. Nae Nae and Stevie came in ahead of their mother and made a beeline for the tiny kitchen.

"Kylie, we're back!" Stevie announced.

"I see."

"What're you cookin'?" Nae Nae asked.

"Grandma's chicken soup," Kylie said.

"We're not going to be late for the puppet show, are we?" Stevie asked. His large brown eyes peered worriedly around the kitchen at the dinner preparations.

"No," Kylie said as she scooped him up, "we're going to be early!"

Stevie smiled and threw his arms around her neck.

"I'll watch the soup for you while you're gone," Jillian said.

"All right. Thanks, Mama." Kylie checked her watch. It was still twenty minutes before the puppet show began at the library around the corner. But if they got there early they could look for a couple of books and get good seats. Kylie went to get her coat.

"Oh, Mama," Kylie said as she slipped her arms into her coat. "Can I go out Tuesday night with this boy named Ian Striver?" Kylie had never been out on a date; she wasn't quite sure how her mother would react. Jillian wasn't strict, and tended not to make a big deal of things, still. . . .

"Who is he?"

"He's a junior at Cross."

"Where are you talking about going?" Jillian asked. She had stopped cleaning up the kitchen and stood still, giving Kylie her undivided attention.

"Just to get something to eat, hang out, you know. No big deal."

"Well, all right. I want to meet him when he comes to pick you up."

"Okay," Kylie said as she tried to conceal her sigh of relief. "See you later, Mama. And thank you."

"You're welcome."

Kylie headed out the door with the kids, all of them dressed for the cold December day. Jillian stood watching her children walk away from her, the icy winter wind whisking the scarves of the two small ones into the air. Jillian had never heard Kylie mention an Ian Striver before. Boys rarely called there at all. Now a date, seemingly out of the blue. It made Jillian pause. But she wasn't the type to make a big deal out of nothing. She could wait and see.

Chapter 5

Ian sat in Michael's basement with the old members and new pledges of FBI. The basement was spacious and comfortable and ESPN was tuned to a college basketball game between Duke and North Carolina.

"So, we need to go over some things," Dante Harris began. Dante was a senior at Cross and president of FBI. He was fine with a muscular build, light complexion, dark eyes, and curly hair styled in a small Afro. "The talent show is a little more than two weeks away and we have to be on point."

"No doubt," Ian concurred.

"So Ian, is your routine all set?" Dante asked.

"No, but it's getting there." This was true. Ian practiced

with Zaire and Tamar, his backup singers, and the keyboard player, Marcus Shipp, at least three times a week.

"Cool. Why don't you let us check out what you got right now?" Michael asked.

"No problem," Ian said. "Come on, y'all." Ian, Zaire, and Tamar stood up together, and the other boys settled back to watch and listen. The three sang with an easy, confident grace, their voices like velvet, particularly Ian's.

"Yeah, that's tight," Michael said.

"I saw you all practicing your routine last Friday," Carlos said. "It's sweet as hell!"

"Yeah, I know," Michael said with a smile. The rest of FBI was entering the contest with a dance and jit routine. It was high energy and complex because there was actually a clever little skit played out with the dance. The music was a mix CD of popular dance and R&B tunes that would be sure to get the audience hyped. In addition, Sean's oldest brother worked at Chene Park, a popular concert venue in Detroit, and he could get them some smoke machines and special lighting effects. "But Brandon Gipson and them probably have a routine that'll give us a run for our money." The other boys nodded in agreement. "All that said, I still don't plan to lose to them, or anybody else. Well, maybe to our own boys here," Michael said, giving Ian a play.

"So how are the challenges coming?" Dante said looking over the new recruits. During the initiation period new FBI pledges had to complete at least three challenges. Ian's first challenge was to come up with four hundred dollars for a party that the FBI was giving at a hall on the west side of town. He'd done that by getting his sister to loan him a hundred, swindling a fifty-dollar gift out of his grandmother—he still felt a little guilty about that one—talking his father into two hundred for Sean John hookups he'd never purchased, and withdrawing fifty out of his savings account without his mother's knowledge.

His second challenge had been to go over to Windsor, Ontario, just fifteen minutes away in Canada, and buy eleven maple leaf–decorated shot glasses with which the eleven FBI members could toast their general greatness. It wasn't too difficult a challenge, in theory. When he left home that night at nine o'clock he figured that it would actually be fun, since he was picking up Sean, Carlos, and Tamar for company. But Carlos forgot his passport and didn't realize it until after they'd been in the slow-moving inspection line for forty-five minutes. So they'd had to drive twenty minutes back to his home on the northeast side of Detroit, then return to start all over again in the line.

Then Tamar, who'd been told too many times by the wrong people that he was funny, decided to crack a weed joke to the border control guards, who politely but sternly directed Ian to pull over. He told all of them to follow him inside a small building, where he proceeded to interrogate them for thirty-five minutes while three other guards inspected Ian's ride. The guard asked where they were going ("nowhere, just hanging out," it seems, is not a satisfactory answer); how long they'd be staying ("about an hour" sounds like just enough time to conduct several illegal drug transactions); and how old they were (they discovered that sixteen is always a highly unacceptable age to be).

Somehow they managed to get out of the station without their parents being called, but a two-hour trip that began at nine o'clock didn't end until nearly 3 A.M.

When Ian returned with the shot glasses, FBI members cracked up as he and the other pledges told the story.

Now Ian was on his final challenge, and it was the most difficult of all. This one depended so much on somebody else: the girl . . . this Kylie. Would she like him? Would she like him enough? Could he get some kind of proof of how much she liked him to bring back to an FBI meeting? Ian shook his head in puzzlement. Though Michael had handed out the challenge casually, almost impulsively, at the winter dance, it was now a very real fact of Ian's life. And it was a problem. If Ian didn't complete all of his challenges he would likely be dropped from FBI, and everything he'd worked so hard for over the past few months would have been for nothing. So the only thing to do was to complete this challenge successfully *and* on time. Period.

Ian listened as Carlos told the guys about his challenge to juggle two of the finest girls at school for fifteen days without either one finding out, or dumping him if they did find out. Then he had to get rid of them on day sixteen, even if he really liked one or both by then. Sean's last challenge was to steal five things that totaled over five hundred dollars in value over the next three weeks and turn them in to the fraternity. Tamar's final challenge was to hack into the school's computer system and do some creative grade changes.

Then it was Ian's turn to report on his progress. "Not

too much to tell so far," Ian said. "I've got the girl, thanks to Mike."

"Yeah, I did the best I could for you, too," Mike said with a laugh.

"Yeah, right," Ian said. "Anyway, like I said, I've got the girl picked out, I've got her number, I've talked to her on the phone, and now I've got a date."

"All right, that's straight," Dante said. "Mike says she's a bow-wow, Ian. That right?"

"Yeah, a little. She's all right, I guess." The fellas chuckled.

"But she ain't no Tricia, huh, man?" Dante asked with a knowing smile.

"Ain't too much of nobody a Tricia, man," Ian said. "All those curves, that face and hair, and the way she knows how to work it all? Naw, this girl sure as hell ain't no Tricia."

"Man, I know y'all got some hard-ass challenges, but Ian might just have the hardest, 'cause he's got to screw a dog!" Mike hollered. At that, all of the boys fell out laughing and giving one another plays, Ian right along with them. This is what he'd wanted. He had been popular before, but FBI gave him a brotherhood. Now he was included in this group of jokes, laughter, secrets, popularity, and he had the right to walk the halls of Cross like a damn prince!

All he had to do was keep it.

When Ian got home that night he yelled hi to his mother and sister, then went directly upstairs. He wanted to get a little homework in before it got to be too late.

"Ian," Ms. Striver called upstairs twenty minutes later.

"Yeah, Ma."

"Come on down here and get something to eat."

Ian came down the stairs and into the kitchen. "What is this?" Ian said in surprise. "You cooked dinner?"

"Okay, knucklehead, enough with the sarcasm. You want some or what?"

"When I smelled all this good food, I thought you were heating up some carryout from a restaurant."

"So what do you want?"

"Whatta you got?" Ian asked interested.

"Baked chicken, greens, macaroni and cheese, corn bread, fried squash, fried corn, gravy, and fruit punch."

"Dang, woman, you *do* love us, don't you?" Ian said as he wrapped his arms around his mother and kissed her cheek.

"You," she said kissing him back, "are a silly, silly boy." She fixed his plate, and he sat down with his sister and mother and had a delicious home-cooked meal with music, laughter, and talk. It had been a while since they'd done this together, but that wasn't important, at the moment. The good company they shared now, was.

Chapter 6

Tuesday evening Kylie stood at the kitchen window, gently biting her lower lip. She lived in one of the small but proudly maintained homes in the Ralph Bunche co-ops. They'd been on a wait list for three years to get into the pretty community. The kitchen window faced the parking lot. Ian was supposed to come in ten minutes and Kylie had already made up her mind that he probably wouldn't show.

Her mama's old black Honda Accord sat parked directly in front of their place as it usually did. The two spots adjacent to the Accord were empty. Empty and waiting, it seemed. "It's early," Kylie whispered to the worried parking spaces. He was due to arrive at 5 P.M. and already the sun was well into its descent. The sky, bleak all day, pitiless as a sheet of steel, pulled its cloak of shadow about itself. A cold wind bit across the landscape, and the parking lot was still. No one seemed willing to brave the cold and comfortless vista. Kylie worried that Ian would feel that a date with her wasn't worth coming out into such an evening.

She went to the mirror in the dining room and checked herself again. She wore faded jeans and an oversized blue sweater with a white T-shirt showing at its V-neck. She thought that she looked okay but her hair, again, betrayed her. She'd shampooed and blow-dried it and curled it under. But it had too many split ends and the whole cut was uneven and lifeless-looking. Kylie sighed and turned away from the mirror.

The girls that she saw Ian with at school had the latest haircuts, the sweetest designer clothes and shoes, gold jewelry, and a perfect sense of style. They carried small leather purses that held money and cell phones, and, she thought glumly, the secrets to being popular and noticed. Those girls drew boys like Ian to them like the moon pulled the tides of the sea.

Kylie had already spent an hour helping Nae Nae with her third-grade language arts assignment. Now the kids were coloring at the table and Jillian was curled up on the couch reading a murder mystery. The aroma of her mother's baked chicken, mashed potatoes, gravy, and sweet peas still hung in the air an hour after dinner.

Everything seemed calm and pleasant, a sharp contrast to the tension building up inside of Kylie. Despite the cool conversation that she had had with Ian yesterday she could see all sorts of ways this evening could go wrong. While she didn't know why Ian was interested in seeing her, she knew why she wanted to see him: he made her insides flutter. She liked the look of him and the way his voice sounded. When he had danced with her Friday night she'd enjoyed his nearness, and wanted more of it.

She was so caught up in these thoughts that for a moment she hardly noticed the dark blue Capri pull into one of the parking spaces next to her mother's car. She jumped slightly when she woke to the reality before her.

"He's here. Now, just say hello and then let him be," Kylie reminded her brother and sister.

"All right," Nae Nae said.

"Kylie has a lover boy," Stevie whispered with a grin.

"He is not my lover boy, and for God's sake, don't say anything like that when he gets in here. He's not my boyfriend, okay?"

"Okay," he said. Stevie was a little alarmed by the urgency in his sister's voice. Kylie was usually so calm and collected. Stevie stopped grinning and got a little nervous himself. Then Nae Nae leaned over and nudged him playfully and he relaxed a little. "I'm sorry," he said to Kylie.

"Oh, no, it's all right, sweetie. I'm sorry I snapped at you." She stooped to give him a quick hug, and the doorbell rang just as she released him. Jillian uncurled her legs and slipped her feet into her fuzzy, pale-blue house shoes. She marked her page with a bookmark.

"All right," Kylie said looking at her mother.

"All right," Jillian said, offering Kylie what she hoped was a reassuring smile.

Kylie opened the door to find Ian standing there with his hands inside the pockets of his brown leather coat and his hazel eyes gazing directly into hers.

"What's up?" Ian said. And then he smiled, and Kylie thought surely he must hear this singing inside of her. Everyone must hear it.

"Hi," she said, smiling back. "Come on in."

Ian stepped inside and Kylie closed the door behind him, shutting out the cold.

"Hello," Jillian said from the couch, "I'm Ms. Winship."

"How are you today?" Ian asked.

"Oh, I'm well enough," Jillian said. "How about yourself?"

"I'm pretty good, thank you," Ian said politely. He said "Hi," to Nae Nae and Stevie.

"So what are your plans for this evening, Ian?" Jillian asked. Kylie put on her coat while they talked.

"I thought that we'd drive out to Sheldon and get something to eat, then hang out at the laser tag place out there for a while. You know, if that's all right with you and Kylie."

"That sounds fine," Jillian said.

Ian looked over at Kylie to see what she thought, and she nodded yes.

"Well, you all better get going then. Be back by nine o'clock, Kylie, you two have school tomorrow," Jillian said.

"Okay." Kylie said. Then she gave both her sister and brother a quick kiss on the cheek. Jillian stood, ready to see the two of them out the door.

"You ready?" Ian asked her.

"Yes. Bye, Mama," Kylie said.

"Bye, Kylie." Ian and Kylie stepped into the evening and Jillian shut the door behind them.

Ian headed to his side of the car and Kylie to the passenger side. After unlocking his door, Ian hit the power locks and Kylie climbed in. Ian got in and started the car, and the heaters flooded the small car with warmth. A popular rapper filled the air with his rhythmic sound. Without a word, Ian backed out of the parking space and they were off.

Kylie sat beside him nervously, liking the music but too self-conscious to even nod her head to the beat. Ian gripped the steering wheel with one hand and allowed his head to bob up and down, up and down as they sped along the street. Kylie wanted to look at him, but she didn't want him to see her do it, so she sat stiffly, looking straight ahead, barely seeing what they were passing. They were soon out of her eastside Detroit neighborhood, and on the expressway, one of thousands of darkened vessels bejeweled by red, yellow, and white lights. She wished that he'd say something.

Less than twenty minutes later they were in the nearby town of Sheldon, cruising down its quiet streets where the shops, restaurants, and cafés were warmly lit and inviting. She'd filled the time in the car imagining all of the things she *would* say. In her imagination she was incredibly witty and smooth.

When he spoke she was startled back into her anxiety. "We're here."

She looked more carefully out of the window. They were parked in front of a row of stores, a café, and a Coney

Island restaurant flooded with bright lights at the end of the block.

When they got out of the car the cold air hit Kylie hard. She pulled her hood over her head and pressed her hands into her pockets. Ian was waiting for her when she rounded the front of the car and they walked side by side. When they got to the café they were both drawn by the jazz notes filtering out on the night air, and they looked in to see the pleasant glow of the lights, the cozy tables, the busy waitstaff.

"You want to check this out?" Ian asked.

"Sure," she said and he opened the door for her. Inside it was warm and deliciously aromatic. The scent of smoked sausages, chili, French fries, hamburgers, and rich coffees floated in the air. Nearly every table was occupied, and a small jazz band was in full swing on a slightly raised platform. Kylie liked the place immediately. "It's nice," she said.

"Yeah."

"Hi," a redheaded young woman said. She smiled cheerfully, and Kylie couldn't help but smile back. "Two?"

They followed her to a tiny table that had a clear view of the band and most of the café. Kylie eased out of her coat, all the while looking around her and avoiding eye contact with Ian. The walls held framed posters of city and countryside scenes of Italy, France, Germany, Switzerland, Brazil, Egypt, Canada, and the U.S. There was a bar that served coffee and a kitchen not far from their table.

"You're quiet," Ian observed.

"You too."

He smiled. "Yeah. So how are you?"

"I'm fine. How are you?"

"I'm tight. Are you hungry?"

"Not really. I ate dinner already."

"Oh. I'm starving." Ian picked up one of the menus that sat on the table and began looking it over. After about a minute he set it aside.

"So, what are you getting?" Come on, Kylie urged herself, try.

"A smoked sausage and fries."

"That sounds good."

"If you want something, just let me know." Kylie noticed that he was looking around the restaurant as he made the offer. His disinterest irritated her, even as she told herself that she shouldn't let it.

"Well, I'll have a peach cobbler and a hot cocoa, then."

Ian looked at her and nodded. When the waitress came they placed their orders then settled back to listen to the music and look around.

"The music's good," Ian said.

"Yeah. Do you play any instruments?"

"The piano a little. I always wanted to play really well, but I've never had lessons."

"You should take a class at Cross."

"My schedule is always too full. Do you play an instrument?"

"Yeah, the thigh."

"What?" Ian leaned in closer to hear her better.

Kylie smiled. "The thigh." She slapped her thigh to the jazz band's beat. "You know."

"I like to play the thigh, too," he said, his eyes holding hers. They both laughed, Kylie's giggle a little nervous.

After that they relaxed some and talked. The time clipped away and the air between them became easy and pleasant, like the music and the food. The warmth and flavor of the room seeped inside of them and came out in their words and laughter.

Kylie felt good. This is how she had hoped things would go. She was glad that they'd ended up at the café, it was more intimate, grown-up, and romantic than the Coney Island restaurant and laser tag would have been. After a while she checked her watch and it was 8 P.M.

"You ready to get out of here? We could drive around for a little while before I take you back," Ian said as he paid the bill.

"Yeah, okay," Kylie said. They got back into their coats and pulled on their hats and gloves. Outside the temperature had dropped a few degrees and the clouds had been blown away to reveal a sky enchantingly dark and wide, pierced by the occasional sharp, bright star. Kylie paused outside the door and breathed deeply.

Ian looked up where Kylie looked, then looked at her. "Pretty," he said softly.

"Yes," Kylie said, gazing into his eyes by the light that shone from the café window. After the sweet rhythm of the evening she felt like kissing him under the lovely night sky.

"Let's get you out of the cold," Ian said. They hurried to the car and got in, greeted by the chill interior. Ian started up the car and they sat silently as it warmed up. "God, it's cold," he said. Kylie nodded. It wasn't long, though, before the car had warmed up some and Ian pulled out into traffic.

R&B music played as the air warmed around them and Ian cruised easily down the road, headed nowhere in particular. Kylie felt comfortable and languid. She didn't feel any pressure to talk, nothing like the nervous silence at the beginning of their date. She had carefully tucked away any concerns about why Ian might have invited her out. Right now she had what she wanted, the warm attentions of a boy she liked and an evening when she got to be a sixteen-year-old, hanging out and free of care.

After a while they were back in Detroit, and Ian pulled onto Belle Isle. The island was about six square miles, surrounded by the Detroit River and approached by a quarter-mile-long, beautiful white bridge. The island was composed of patches of woods, grass, ponds, picnic areas, and winding roads that made a pleasant place for families, couples, and friends to hang out. They watched the Canadian skyline across the Detroit River as they cruised around the island. Tonight the river was a dark ribbon, still along the edges where the water had frozen over, and laboriously in motion through the middle where the cold, cold water marked a slow path. On the interior of the path, trees crowded together for warmth and created dark smudges against the blue-black sky. It wasn't long before Ian had parked the car facing the water and the Canadian skyline.

The car hummed quietly beneath them as they bobbed their heads gently to the music.

"Are you going to be in the talent contest this year?"

Kylie asked Ian. The winter talent show was in six weeks.

"Yeah. One of my boys is going to play the keyboard while I sing lead and two of my boys sing backup." He sat facing forward, tapping the steering wheel with his fingertips as he spoke. "It should be tight. He can really play."

"Who's that?"

"Marcus Shipp. You know him?"

"No."

"Oh. Well, he's been playing the piano since he was five and he started playing the keyboard when he was around nine or something. He's bad."

"Sounds like he would be. A prodigy or something."

"Yeah, he is. Are you coming to the show?"

"Yes. I know some people who are gonna be in it."

"Like me," he said smiling at her.

"Yeah, like you now."

"Do you want to get out and look at the sky again?"

"Sure. That would be nice."

Outside the wind held itself still as Ian circled around his car and stood beside Kylie. They gazed at the sky and Kylie felt the solidness of the earth beneath her feet, and the chill against her cheek, comforting reminders that she was really there and that this night with Ian was real.

"I've had a really good time with you tonight," Ian said. "I'm glad we never made it to laser tag." He stood before her now, near and enticing. Kylie already knew that she would not satisfy her urge to kiss him. That would be too ridiculous. It would ruin everything to step out on such a limb and feel it crack and break beneath her feet. Better to stay here on the ground, where she was safe.

"Me, too," she answered softly. His eyes looked thoughtful and confused. And then he was drawing his face close to hers and her breath caught in her throat as she realized that he was going to kiss her. Her mouth went instantly and dramatically dry, and she was flooded by the fear that she was about to deliver a kiss as dry as the Sahara to a boy as fine as Ian. But before she completed that train of thought his lips were against hers. To her surprise, they were warm and tender. Somehow, fleetingly, she had thought that his lips would be cold from the night air. She heard the gentle *whoosh* of the sleeves of his coat as he moved his hands from his pockets to her arms. She felt his mouth open over hers, unhurried and sure, and without thinking she was French-kissing him back. She felt the gentle languidness inside of her give way to a thrilling hum and she thought, Ian is the sweetest kisser I have ever known.

When they pulled apart it took her a while to feel the earth beneath her feet and the chill air upon her cheek. At first she could only feel the pull of the earth spinning. And it was several moments longer before she realized that it was not the world's spinning that she felt, but the spinning of a new world inside of her.

She was even less prepared for his second kiss. But it came, as sweet, and then sweeter than the first.

As they drove toward her home Kylie thought that as much as she had enjoyed the night so far, she had wondered where they could meet together comfortably, with something in common. She was neither a performer like him, nor was she popular. He knew nothing about taking care of younger siblings, preparing meals, or being a part-time "mother." They had no friends in common; they didn't hang out at the same places.

It was here, she realized. Here in these kisses they were perfectly matched.

Less than fifteen minutes after kissing her Ian pulled out of Kylie's parking lot and into the little traffic that moved down her street toward the freeway. He tried to empty his mind, but instead, Kylie remained in his thoughts. When he'd picked her up he'd felt stiff and kind of uncomfortable. He'd been in her home, meeting her mother, sister, and brother, and he was basically planning to play her to the left. As he was at other times with other girls, he was polite, but his motives were all messed up. The thought of it irritated him so much that he had barely been able to open his mouth during the ride to Sheldon.

Then there was that whole Sheldon thing, he thought with a grimace. He had driven all the way out there because he didn't want anyone to see him with Kylie. She wasn't cute or cool enough for him to go out with. It wasn't fair, and it might not be right, in some people's eyes. And while he could admit this to himself, still there it was, a fact of life.

But, he'd liked her! Ian thought in frustration. She was easy to talk to, and she could be funny. And that kiss . . .

He had kissed her because it was part of the plan. He

couldn't very well get her to sleep with him in just a few weeks without getting her to think that he liked her. So, he knew he had to kiss her tonight. At the café as they'd talked and laughed together, he had begun to warm up to her. At that point he still wasn't all that attracted to her. But the way that she'd looked at him before he kissed her made him pause. He could see right there in her face that she liked him, and that did something to him. And the way that she had kissed him back . . . he had to stop to relish the thought. The kiss was so good, it was like she was handing him something precious. "Damn," he whispered aloud. The second kiss he gave without even thinking. He had *wanted* to kiss her.

"Just do this and be done with it," he mumbled. He would never have Kylie for a girlfriend. Never. She would never fit in with FBI, and he would never give up FBI for a girl.

Chapter 7

Wednesday afternoon found Ian rapping lightly on his guidance counselor's door as he headed down the main hallway on his way home. "What's up, Mr. Hill?"

"Hey, Ian? How are your classes going?"

"All right. You know," Ian said. He leaned against the door frame. Mr. Hill was his favorite adult at school. He was honest and real, and he spoke to students like young adults, not as though they were the enemy, to be handled and controlled.

"No, I don't know. Why don't you tell me?"

"Pretty good. I'm trying harder. You saw my last report card."

"Yes. You've gone up a couple of points. But you're still

not really pushing yourself, Ian. You're going to have to show significant improvement if you want any good schools to give you a chance next year."

Ian knew Mr. Hill was right, but he didn't feel like getting into some heavy discussion right now. He had enough on his mind. "You're right, Mr. Hill, you are most definitely right. Look, I'll come by next week so we can talk some more."

"All right, Ian. Make sure that you do that."

"Bet. Take it easy, Mr. Hill."

"You too, Ian."

The rest of the school day was typical. He hung with his friends, went to class, checked out the girls, and squeezed up on Tricia a little bit. But off and on all day he had had to fight off thoughts of Kylie and the time they'd spent together the night before. Once, in civics, he actually lost track of what was going on because he was thinking about what it felt like to kiss her.

So, try as he might to resist, he wasn't exactly surprised when he found himself going out of his way to cruise by her locker at the end of seventh hour. But, he lied to himself, he could go up there and see if Ms. Lyndon was around and check out his average in Algebra III. When Ian rounded the corner near Kylie's locker and saw her standing there alone, getting her things out to go home, he mentally kicked himself for being so excited. She looked up and smiled when she saw him coming.

"What's up?" Ian greeted her.

"Hey, Ian."

"You headed home?"

"Yeah, but I'm not in a hurry." As if to prove her point she turned and leaned with her back against the locker next to hers. "What about you?"

"Yeah, in a little while. I'm not in a hurry, either."

"Thanks again for last night. I had a really good time," Kylie said.

"Me, too. You want to hook up again?"

Kylie was surprised, but she hoped that she hid it well. "Sure."

"Cool," Ian said with a small smile. "What about Sunday? We could check out a movie or something." He figured few people he knew would be at the movies on Sunday night.

"Uhmm, I don't know," Kylie said. "We have school the next day and I have homework to do. I have to help out with my brother and sister, and stuff, too."

"Oh, yeah, I understand. . . ."

"But you could come over my house. That is, if you want. We could do homework together, or something."

Her expression crumbled when Ian teased her with a look that said "Are you crazy?" "No, no," he said hurriedly, "I'm just messin' with you. That would be cool. What time?"

"Five-thirty?"

"Yeah, five-thirty works. I'll see you then," he said and headed down the hall.

"All right."

"Ian," she called when he was a little way off.

"Yeah?"

"Come here a second." When he stood before her again she looked up into his eyes, which seemed even more golden just then, and swallowed. "You never gave me your number."

"You never asked for it."

"Oh," she said blushing.

"Well?" he teased.

"Can I have your number?"

"Absolutely," he said with a smile that made her melt inside. Then he leaned over and whispered it, his lips grazing her ear slightly. He got her so caught up she hoped that she'd be able to remember the number. When he was done he smiled and walked away.

After he'd rounded the corner Kylie hurried up and scribbled it down in one of her spirals before she had a chance to forget it. She was actually humming when she heard a pleasant, familiar voice behind her.

"What's up, Kylie?"

Kylie turned around to find Terrance Wells behind her. Terrance was tall and well built with an athlete's grace, warm brown skin, attractive features, and a generous smile. "What's up, Terrance?"

"Nothing. I was just wondering how you were doing in Algebra III?"

"That class is kicking my butt. What about you?"

"I'm doing pretty good," Terrance said. "Maybe we can hook up and I can tutor you."

"Sure."

"Cool. What's your free hour?"

"Fourth. What's yours?"

"I have study hall fourth hour, so that would be all right. And I'm sure the teacher would let you come up there if he saw that I was helping you."

"All right. Why are you being so nice to me?" she asked lightly.

Terrance smiled shyly as he answered, "Because, you know, I am good at math, so . . ." He ended with a shrug.

"Well, thanks." Kylie put on her coat and picked up her book bag.

"No problem." He shifted his books to his other hand. "Well, how about Monday?"

"Monday's good."

"Bet." He transferred his books back to his right hand. "See you later, Kylie," Terrance said as he left.

"Bye." Kylie watched Terrance go down the hallway for a few moments. Two boys dropped by my locker in the same day! I haven't had two boys at my locker in the same *year* since I've been here, she thought with some surprise. Go figure.

By the time she was ready to go, Tracy and Dez were arriving at their own lockers, which were on either side of hers.

"You're not leaving, are you?" Tracy asked. Her perfectly cut short hairstyle looked good, and she managed to pull off a low-key, casual chic in her tight jeans and snug sweater that Kylie wasn't quite able to master.

"No, I was going to wait on you."

"So what's up?" Dez wore her long, dark hair in a ponytail today and as usual she looked pretty.

"Ian stopped by." Kylie had already told her friends all about her date with Ian on Tuesday.

"Here?" Dez asked.

"Yeah. We might get together over my house to do homework." Dez and Tracy looked at the shy, pleased look on their friend's face and exchanged glances.

"Is that right?" Tracy said lightly.

"I told him I'd have to check. But my mother should say yes if I take care of all my chores."

"Sounds straight," Tracy said.

"Yeah," Dez added. "Well, I'm ready. Let's go."

The other two girls hoisted their backpacks onto their shoulders and the three started out of the building and toward Desiree's car. Before long they arrived at Kylie's place. "Well, see you," Kylie said.

"All right, girl," Tracy said.

"Yeah, peace, little sis," Dez said.

"So what do you think?" Tracy asked Dez, once Kylie was in the door and they drove away.

"About Ian and Kylie?" Dez asked.

"Yeah. What's that all about?"

"Girl, you got me. I know that it's all of a sudden."

"Yeah, and weird," Tracy said. "I mean, we know how cool Kylie is. But Ian and his boys have never given her the time of day. Now all of a sudden Ian is calling her, taking her out, stopping by her locker. . . . What is up with that?" Tracy looked worriedly at Dez.

"I don't know. But I don't have a good feeling about it."

"Me either. Remember that stuff that was going around about Ian last year?"

"What?" Dez asked.

"That he dogged girls, mainly. People were saying how he would sleep with these girls and then dump them."

"Yeah, I remember now. That was messed up. One of the girls was talking about having her older brother and cousins jump him."

"Yep," Tracy said. They sat quietly for a few minutes. "Well, Kylie's a virgin. So we shouldn't have to worry about him going around saying that he slept with her."

"Great logic, Tracy," Dez said wryly. "Have you seen Ian lately? He is fine as hell. Have you paid attention to Kylie's face every time she's mentioned him? She lights up, big light-bulb action there."

"So?"

"So, things can change. What's to stop Kylie from having sex with Ian?"

"Common sense, I hope!"

"Look, I'm not trying to diss our girl, but if her common sense were working at this time, we wouldn't even have to discuss this."

"What do you mean?"

"I mean, and again, I'm not trying to diss Kylie, but why would someone like Ian be into her? She's not what he likes, and he ain't got sense enough to see what she has to offer on the inside. Something is up."

"You're right," admitted Tracy slowly.

"I'll tell you this," Desiree said with a sudden and fiery

light in her eyes, "if Ian hurts her, I'm going to make sure he pays."

"Now, hold up, Dez. It's not like that yet. We don't even know if it will *ever* be like that."

"I do, though. I wish that I didn't, but I do. I just feel it." The girls rode in silence for a bit.

"What do we tell Kylie?" Tracy wondered.

"The truth. The truth is going to be her best defense when things go down."

"If. If things go down," said Tracy.

"How are you, Ian?" his father asked.

"I'm all right, Dad. How are you?" Ian held the phone to his ear with his shoulder while he ironed his shirt for the next day. He stood in a T-shirt and boxer shorts and had a rerun of *My Wife and Kids* turned down low.

"Oh, pretty good. Kelsey has a bad cold and it's keeping everyone up at night. She coughs and wakes up, and then she cries, so Miranda and I get up, too."

"Oh," Ian said. He wasn't all that interested in his father's other kid's cold.

"Well, I'm not going to bore you with all of the details," his father said with a little chuckle, almost as though he sensed Ian's thoughts. "How is school going?"

"All right."

"What kind of grades do you have right now?"

"A couple of B's, a couple of C's, one A, and I don't know what I have in civics."

"That's not too bad, Ian. But it's still way below what you *can* do," his father answered.

"I'm working at it. Hey, I've got a talent show coming up in a few weeks. Do you think you can come and check it out?"

"When is it exactly?"

Ian told him the exact date and time.

"I don't know. I think that Kelsey has a dance recital that day. Let me check with Miranda and see."

"Sure," Ian said, swallowing his disappointment. If it was between little Kelsey's recital and Ian's talent show there was no real competition. His only chance of catching his father was if Kelsey's recital fell on another day.

"I'll try to make it, though. What are you going to do? Dance, sing, what?"

"I'm singing lead with this group that I'm in."

"You always could sing, boy," his father said proudly. "It's been a while since I heard you perform."

After hearing his father's tone of voice, Ian thought, maybe there was some hope.

"Is your sister home?" Mr. Striver asked.

"Yeah, hold up, I'll get her for you," Ian said.

"Take care of yourself," said his father.

"You too," Ian said, before yelling for Kim to pick up.

His father sounded okay, he might actually come through and show up at the talent show. His father had a series of no-shows under his belt where Kim and he were concerned even before he had gotten with Miranda. He had missed more than a few little-league football games, plays, and dance recitals. There was always something to do at work, or some project around the house that needed his father's attention more than they did. Other times it was some friend who needed Mr. Striver to help out with something, or some rest that he just *had* to catch up on because he'd been so busy lately.

The thing was, Ian couldn't hate his father, and it was hard to even seriously dislike him. He was always really apologetic when he let you down, and he was also charming as hell. For years Ian had believed that his father would do better, follow through more often, because he was just so sincere and believable. But by the time he was twelve, Ian had wised up and found it safer to expect little and be pleasantly surprised when he did come through for him or his sister. Still, sometimes he could slip one over on Ian if he wasn't careful.

Chapter 8

"Kick it, kick it, yeah, yeah! Kick it, kick it, yeah, yeah!" The singer on the radio sang with the fast beat, making Kylie's head bounce and her fingers pop. She was arranging her books, paper, spirals, and pens on a table in the basement. Ian would be here shortly and she was excited. Her mother had been fine with Ian coming over to do homework. Jillian didn't tell Kylie, but she was relieved to have them stay at the house so that she could look Ian over more carefully. He and Kylie had talked on the telephone several times since their date and Jillian wanted to know more about this boy who Kylie was so interested in. It was clear to Jillian that her daughter really liked Ian. But quite frankly, Jillian's first impression of him was that he was a bit too smooth for her

Kylie. She'd have to give him a second, more thorough examination this evening.

Kylie checked the basement. It looked fine. There was the card table she and her brother and sister used for studying and to do homework on. Instead of the harsh overhead light, both lamps were lit—one on an end table by an old brown couch, the other on the card table. The large, comfortable beige chair that they usually had clean laundry piled on was cleared and the area where her brother and sister's toys were kept was reasonably neat. The TV was turned off and the boom box just kept telling Kylie to "Kick it, kick it, yeah, yeah!"

Kylie bounded up the stairs and checked the kitchen. She'd rushed through her chores so she would be done well before Ian got here. The first floor was vacuumed and tidy, and meat loaf was reheating in the oven. She'd cooked it yesterday, and so it was leftovers for today. She'd made mashed potatoes, green beans, tossed salad, and biscuits to go with it—so dinner was all set. She'd be able to chill with Ian downstairs while her family ate upstairs. They had chips and Faygo soda to offer Ian. She debated whether or not to bring the snacks down in advance and decided not to. She didn't want it to seem like she thought this was any big deal. Having the snacks laid out like a little party seemed lame.

"Relax, Kylie," Jillian said when she came into the small kitchen.

"I am relaxed."

"You don't look it," Jillian said dryly.

"What are Nae Nae and Stevie doing?"

"Finishing their homework."

"Oh."

"Well, you two behave down there."

"We will, Mama. We're just doing homework. That's all."

"All right, now. Just make sure. I was sixteen once."

"Yes, Mama," Kylie said smiling. Just then the doorbell rang.

"I'll get it," Jillian said.

"Okay," Kylie stayed in the kitchen. Just like that her insides felt strung tight.

"Hi, Ms. Winship," she heard Ian say. A wisp of cold air curled itself around the corner of the kitchen and kissed her ankles.

"Hello, Ian. Come on in," her mother invited him.

Kylie came out of the kitchen to stand in the dining room. He smiled when he saw her.

"Hi, Ian." Kylie knew she ought to be saying something more, but for the life of her she couldn't think of what it was. The quiet grew a tiny bit uncomfortable and Jillian coughed.

"You two go on to the basement to study," Jillian said.

"Yes," Kylie said with a shake of her head. "Let's go downstairs." Ian just smiled and followed her.

"I'll go hang up your coat," Kylie realized that she'd forgotten to offer to take it when he came in. Chill, girl, she urged herself.

"Thanks," Ian said as he shrugged it off. He handed it to her and she tried to calmly and gracefully walk up the stairs to hang it up, while feeling his eyes on her. When she got back Ian was sitting on the couch, the books and folder that he'd brought were sitting on the table across from her things.

"So what's up?" Ian said when she got downstairs.

"Nothing, you know."

"Thanks for having me over to study."

"You're welcome." She loved his smile. She especially loved having him smile at her.

"Sit here," he said patting the cushion next to him. She sat down, nervous and happy.

"Can I kiss you?" he asked softly. She was looking straight ahead, and he leaned over very close and whispered the words into her ear. She nodded yes.

"Come here," he urged as he turned her head gently by placing his index finger under her chin. He kissed her softly on her closed lips. When he stopped and opened his eyes all he saw were her eyes, her black, black eyes open and staring into his. Ian had tried to tell himself that when he saw Kylie this evening it would be all about business. Kiss her, buzz sweet nothings into her ear, all in a serious effort to get in her panties in just two short weeks. Because that's all that he had left now. He had every intention of meeting this challenge set by Michael and putting another important feather in his cap as a future FBI member who could get things done. That is what he had been telling himself.

But every time that he was busy convincing himself of his motives he had to pause and be honest with himself. He *wanted* to kiss Kylie. He wanted to hold her, and he wanted to spend time with her. It had started during that first tele-phone conversation when time got away from him, and it grew worse when he took her out. If Ian was perfectly honest with himself, he had never had such a good time just hanging with a girl and talking with her. Then when he'd kissed her that night he'd felt as though he'd been snared, caught in some sweet trap.

He knew that he ought to shake these feelings off, but he didn't know how and he wasn't sure that he really wanted to. And he ought to do it before he got into trouble. It wasn't just that he didn't think he *should* be with someone like Kylie, he didn't *want* to be with someone like her. He didn't want a girl-friend with messed-up hair, a plain face, and a bony body. He didn't want a girlfriend that brothers would be teasing him about, or dogging behind his back. He didn't want a girlfriend who was a joke, and he sure as hell didn't want to be a joke himself. He wanted a beautiful girl that other brothers would secretly lust after. And, he reasoned, it would be *good* if she was easy to talk to and laugh with like Kylie was. But if he had to pick either gorgeous and stylish, or plain and great to be with, it would have to be the first. He wasn't proud of this fact, but he was willing to be straight with himself.

So when he kissed her lips and felt his heart reacting and saw her dark eyes melting into his, he felt guilty. He told him-self that it wouldn't hurt anybody too much if he just went ahead and gave them both a little pleasure here, in private, right now. "Come here," he said again as he closed in for another kiss. She came to him easily and willingly, and this time he French-kissed her.

"I love the way you kiss me," Ian whispered, his lips still close to hers.

"Why?"

"Why?" Ian echoed in surprise, leaning back a little. He hadn't expected her to ask why. Who asked why when they were told that they were a good kisser? "Why?"

"Yes. I want you to tell me so that I can do it again, every time," she said.

Ian smiled at her. "Do you say everything that you're thinking?"

"No," Kylie answered, "not everything. But really, tell me why."

"Let me see. Well, your kisses are sweet. You make your lips all soft and easy, and you're never moving your tongue in a hurry. It just feels good," he finished, at a loss. "And you're not spitting all over the place," he added trying to shift to a lighter mood.

Kylie smiled. "Here," she said as she leaned in to kiss him. They moved from one kiss to the next, to the next, and the next before they heard small feet at the top of the stairs.

"Kylie," Stevie said.

"Yeah," Kylie said as she and Ian pulled apart hurriedly.

"Are you going to come have dinner now?" Stevie stood in the middle of the staircase looking at them now.

"No, I'll eat later," Kylie said, not wanting to stop what she and Ian were doing.

"Come on up and eat," Jillian called. "You too, Ian. A bite to eat will do you two some good."

Kylie felt and looked a little frustrated, but Ian only shrugged and smiled good-naturedly.

Upstairs, the circular table was set for five. It looked crowded but welcoming. Saucers of tossed salad and glasses filled with iced tea surrounded the steaming plates of food. The radio dial was set to a station that played a mix of oldies and current hits.

"Everything looks really good, Ms. Winship. Thank you for inviting me to dinner," Ian said.

"Oh, you're welcome. But you better tell Kylie everything looks good, she cooked it."

"For real?" Ian said, looking over at Kylie. She just nodded, embarrassed. She felt like an old woman, coming home and cooking dinner for her family. She wanted to seem lighter, easier, cooler.

They all sat down, Jillian said a simple grace, and everyone started eating. It was quiet at first, except for the usual "pass the salt, please."

"This is really good," Ian said as he looked over at Kylie.

"Yeah?"

"Yes. You can cook. That's straight."

Kylie looked at Ian and realized that he was genuinely appreciative, that he really did like her food *and* thought that it was cool that she could cook. "Thanks, Ian."

"No, thank *you*. My sister and I have to fix most of our meals ourselves. But they're not nearly as good as this. Let's see . . . this week I've had a ham sandwich and chips, two cans of soup another night, and last night my sister and me put on some wing dings and ramen noodles. Believe me, thank you," he said with a grin.

Kylie laughed softly. "You're welcome."

After that they all ate and talked more easily together. Ian helped Kylie, Nae Nae, and Stevie clear the table. He and Kylie packed up the leftover food and put the dishes in hot water to soak. They chatted about nothing in particular and Ian mostly watched the way Kylie moved and handled her sister and brother. She was easy and confident and kind, all without even thinking about it. He felt like kissing her again.

"You wanna play some Uno?" Nae Nae asked Ian as Kylie dried her hands on a dish towel. The kitchen looked neat and orderly and the dishes sat soaking in sudsy water.

"Sure," Ian said.

"Me, too," Stevie called from where he was sitting on the couch with his mother.

"You playing, Mama?" Kylie asked.

"No, you all go ahead," Jillian said as she opened up an espionage thriller. She had decided that though he still bore watching, Ian was okay.

So for the next half an hour they played Uno together. Kylie loved the way that Ian slid into their friendly banter, teasing Nae Nae and Stevie good-naturedly, letting them each win at least once, and humming along to the music. She felt as though her insides were lit up, it was so very, very good. She wanted to jump up and hug him and say "thank you for being so good to my little brother and sister and for chillin' at my home as though it was exactly what you want to do."

"I better go," Ian said after a while. Kylie thought he actually sounded a little disappointed.

"All right," Kylie said.

"Aww," Nae Nae said.

"Naw," Stevie grumbled.

Ian smiled. "Yeah. I'm all full on Kylie's good food, and so relaxed from playing with you all, I probably won't be able to get any more homework done tonight." Kylie blushed at Ian's mention of homework, their "homework" session still fresh in her mind. They put away the cards and Jillian sent Stevie and Nae Nae upstairs to get ready for bed.

Kylie and Ian went downstairs to gather up the homework supplies Ian had never used. "Thanks again for dinner, Kylie," Ian said. "You can really cook."

"You're welcome, and thanks."

"I don't know, that dinner was so good, I should probably give you a better thank-you than that."

"No, that's okay," Kylie said, missing Ian's flirtations.

"No?" he asked and when she looked into his eyes she got it. "No?" he asked again, already lowering his head for the kiss. Kylie wrapped her arms around his neck and allowed him to press her body full against his. She felt his arousal and it excited her to know that she excited him.

"Multitalented," Ian teased when they had finished kissing.

"You, too," Kylie said.

"Well, I better go," he said as he released her. He scooped up his things.

"Okay," Kylie said.

"Can I call you tonight?"

"Yes."

"All right." He turned and headed up the stairs.

Kylie got him his coat, Jillian said good night, and Nae Nae and Stevie yelled good night from upstairs.

Kylie walked him to the door and they had just the tiniest bit of privacy in the darkened doorway. "I'll see you tomorrow," Kylie said in a near whisper.

Ian glanced in Jillian's direction, saw that he couldn't see her, then gave Kylie a quick kiss. "Bye, Ms. Winship."

"Bye, Ian."

Kylie unlocked and opened the door for him. "See you tomorrow, Kylie," Ian said with his hand on the screen door handle.

Then he was out the door and she was shutting it against the December chill.

"So," Jillian began after Ian left, "you really like this boy, huh?"

"I guess," Kylie said evasively. They were finishing up in the kitchen together as Nae Nae and Stevie took turns taking baths upstairs.

"He's nice," Jillian said.

"But?"

"What? I didn't say but," Jillian said.

"No, but I could hear a 'but' in there."

"Okay, *but* be careful."

"Of what?"

"I'm not sure exactly. He seems a little too smooth."

Jillian sounded silly to Kylie. Ian wasn't too smooth. He was fine, popular, easy to talk to, an excellent kisser, and, miracle of miracles, into *her.* "Okay, Mama," Kylie said anyway. It was better to humor her mother and be respectful, than not. "I'll try to be careful."

Chapter 9

Once Ian had gone, Kylie read to Nae Nae and Stevie, then put away her homework after only a few minutes of study. Her thoughts were too occupied with fantasies of Ian to focus on anything like Algebra III. Once the children were asleep and Jillian had gone upstairs to read in bed, Kylie turned the radio to her favorite station, got comfortable on the basement couch, and called Tracy.

"What's up, girl?" Tracy said when she heard her friend on the phone.

"Everything, Tracy, everything!"

"Oh, it's like that? Let me three-way Dez."

"So what's up?" Dez asked once all of the greetings were out of the way.

"I am really falling for Ian Striver!"

"What do you mean *really* falling for him?" Tracy asked as she tried to keep the worry out of her voice. "Like the time you fell for Tony last summer?"

"No, this is different," Kylie said. "That was fun, but this feels so serious."

"Describe serious," Tracy directed.

"We've gone out, we talk on the phone, and we've really connected. And his kisses, girl, they feel like love."

"Maybe you should try to slow it down some, Kylie. At least until you get to know Ian better. Do you remember what happened last year?" Desiree asked.

"What?" Kylie asked.

"People were saying that Ian had sex with girls and then blew them off," Tracy said.

"Yeah, and one of the girls was threatening to have her brother and cousins come up and kick Ian's behind," Dez said.

"To tell the truth, I *had* forgotten about that. But I do remember it now that you bring it up."

"And I heard he's pledging FBI, and you know how scandalous they can be."

"So? That doesn't mean that he's trying to play me."

"Kylie, he's played other girls, though," Tracy said.

"I don't think he'd do me like that," Kylie said.

"Why not?" Tracy asked.

"I think he really likes me."

"I thought you were going to say because you're not going to have sex with him," Desiree said.

"Well, yeah, that too," Kylie said.

"So what makes you think he likes you?" Tracy asked.

"I don't know. It's the way he looks at me sometimes, like after we kiss. And the way that he kisses me, I can feel it. I know that sounds corny, but I can just tell."

"Oh, Kylie!" Dez said unable to keep the exasperation out of her voice. "Just promise me to hold back a little something, okay? I know that that stuff we heard may be rumor, but I got my version from the girl's best friend's cousin directly. So you'd better watch out, or you could be the next star of the Cross rumor show."

"All right. I'll try to be on my toes. But isn't he *fine?*" Kylie asked.

"Yes," Tracy giggled. "He is definitely that."

"I mean those eyes, those lips, shoot, the whole, entire package!" Kylie cooed.

"Yeah, but remember," Dez said in a voice thick with foreboding, "Satan was the most beautiful angel in heaven, and we know how he turned out."

Chapter 10

"You're gonna do fine on the quiz tomorrow," Terrance reassured Kylie. With a quiz coming up on Wednesday they'd decided to meet again after the previous day's tutoring session went so well.

"Thanks to you," Kylie said. "I didn't understand a thing Ms. Hopkins was saying when she went over this stuff. You make it seem simple."

"It is sort of simple."

"Not for me, Terrance. I really appreciate you taking the time to help me," Kylie said. They sat in the back of the study hall, side by side in conjoined desks.

"I'm glad to do it," Terrance said. "We could meet regularly, if you like," he suggested.

"Okay, if it's not too much trouble for you. I could use the help."

"It's not any trouble at all. What days are good for you?"

"I guess Tuesdays and Wednesdays."

"Cool." Terrance watched her put her math book down and take out the novel that she was reading for English class. Kylie looked over at him once she felt his eyes on her. He was not nearly as fine as Ian, but still cute, she thought. She had heard that he was on the baseball team or something, but she wasn't sure.

"Kylie," Terrance began, and then stopped.

"Yeah?"

"Can I have your number? I mean, can I call you sometime?"

She smiled before she could catch herself. The entire time that they had been working she got the sense of some kind of energy just below the surface that she couldn't place or explain. When he asked for her number she realized what it was: Terrance *liked* her. Had he been waiting to ask for her number all this time, she wondered? Is it even possible that she made a boy nervous, even a little? "Yes, and yes."

Terrance smiled back at her. "Okay, bet." He began putting his math material away and she wrote her number down for him inside his spiral. He read it over, while Kylie's thoughts slipped back to Ian and the feel of his lips against hers.

At the end of her day, Kylie headed toward the bank of lockers that Ian shared with a bunch of other popular kids on the third floor. She was nervous and excited. Other than the one class period that she had spent with Terrance and her lunch hour with her friends, Kylie's day had seemed to grind by, a slow slice of boredom that she could not wait to relieve with the spice of Ian's presence. She had halfway expected him to come by her locker or one of her classes during the day. They had had such a good time Sunday night at her house that she hoped he would want to see her as badly as she wanted to see him. But each new class period held the disappointment of his absence. She figured that he must have gotten tied up and decided to walk by his locker and see him.

In French class she had fantasized about how it would be. She would go to Ian and he would see her from a distance. He would be surrounded by his FBI clique and a few girls, but he would catch her eye and maybe he would smile a little. She would smile back at him, unable to hide her shyness. Then he would step around the others and come to stand near her and it would be, suddenly, as though there were no one else but the two of them. They would make plans to talk tonight on the telephone, and maybe they would walk away and find somewhere to kiss privately. She crafted about ten different versions of the fantasy as the end of the school day drew near. She could barely wait to see Ian.

She rounded the southeastern corner of the third floor and saw several FBI guys who'd been at the dance with Ian.

They were bunched together, loud, playful, and stylish. She grew awkward as she noticed several of them looking at her and exchanging glances. She wondered what that was about.

While they were obviously there to attract attention, they were also somehow closed off, especially from people like Kylie. And it was not just that she thought this, it was true, and all the kids knew it—the ones included, and the ones excluded. She hoped that Ian would notice her soon. She didn't want to have to go in among them.

As she got closer to the group Ian and she made eye contact, but he didn't move. Maybe he wanted her to come over to him. Not good, she thought, but okay. But even when she was right up on the group Ian didn't move toward her, acting as though he didn't even see her.

"Hey, Ian," she called.

Ian nodded coolly in Kylie's direction and called, "What's up?" Kylie stopped stepping and tried to gather herself. What was Ian doing? Why was he ignoring her? He couldn't be just blowing her off, she thought. She wasn't going to signal him to come to her, she just wasn't. Besides, she got the distinct impression from his body language and the infuriating way that his eyes skated past her that he wouldn't come anyway. She stood there a few more seconds, waiting awkwardly, then accepting that he was not going to come to her.

As she stood there other people around Ian began to notice her. First was a girl who stood close to his side. She was tall, slim, and curvy. She turned around to say something in Ian's ear and her long, dark hair swung behind her like silk.

Kylie watched as Ian tilted his head to hear what she said, smiled into her eyes, and then shifted his eyes past Kylie again, looking down the hallway in the direction that Kylie had come from.

Kylie swallowed, took one last glance at Ian, and hurried away. She couldn't talk herself out of it—he had ignored her. She felt a lump forming in her throat and her eyes began to sting with unshed tears. Then she got angry. What did she expect to happen, she questioned herself. She knew that it was a long shot for him to like her at all.

She didn't cry. Instead she hurried to her locker, got her things, and hoped that she could catch up to her friends out in the parking lot. She told herself that if she felt miserable it was because she had made the mistake of building up this thing with Ian into something more than it actually was. She didn't have much experience with boys, she didn't really *know* how things went. Boys like Ian probably kissed a lot of girls and all it meant was that they had some fun together. Period. But she wouldn't make the mistake of telling her girls about what just happened. She didn't want to relive it; and they would just give her advice that she might not want to follow, like to leave Ian alone.

What would she do if he called, though? And it was most definitely *if*. What if she had behaved in such an uncool way that he didn't even want to call her again? She wouldn't think about it. Let him call, she prayed, let him call.

Ian watched Kylie hurry down the hall and wanted to call out, "Hold on, let me walk with you." But he didn't, and he knew he wouldn't. He recalled the hurt in her eyes as she stood there and he had to swallow and look away from her receding back.

"Ian, man, ain't that the girl?" Michael asked.

"What girl?" Ian said, stalling.

"You know, man," Michael said, "the one from the winter dance."

"Yeah," Ian said.

"What about her?" Tricia asked. Ian glanced at Tricia, who looked extra fine today, and decided to cut Michael off before he said something stupid.

"Nothing," Ian said.

"Is that your little girlfriend?" Tricia teased. "She's a real cutie."

"Naw, that ain't my girlfriend, but you could be," Ian said as he leaned toward her. Tricia just smiled at Ian and pushed him playfully in his chest.

"Yeah, right. There's no way I want *you* for a boyfriend." But she didn't look the least bit convincing.

"Aw, come on. For you, I'd be willing to change," he teased. Everyone was watching them now.

"Is that right?" she asked.

"Yeah, I think so."

"But what about your little girlfriend who just came by? I don't want to get in her way," she said laughing.

"Yeah, man," Michael piped up, "she's a little 'ruff-ruff' around the edges." He barked the words ruff-ruff. "Just right for a dog like you." Everybody laughed and Ian joined in, too. He didn't think it was funny, and he felt bad for doing it, but he was one of the loudest ones as he slapped Michael a play.

When Kylie got home that evening she was distracted as she went about her normal tasks. Once the kids went to bed she tried to pretend that she hadn't been waiting all evening for Ian to call. She looked at the clock for the thirtieth time and sighed in exasperation when she saw that it was only 8:30 P.M. The tension from today's encounter with Ian had built to such a level of frustration in her that she just had to hear his voice.

She began dialing his number, embarrassed and mad at herself for calling him first after the way that he had behaved. But she kept dialing.

"Hello," a young woman's voice said.

"Hi, may I speak to Ian?"

"Ian isn't here right now, can I take a message?"

"No. Um, well, yeah, tell him Kylie called, please."

"No problem," the young woman said pleasantly.

"Okay, bye," Kylie said weakly.

"Bye," the woman said and hung up.

Kylie placed the phone back on its base, and flung herself backward onto her mother's bed with a huge sigh. "I shouldn't have called," she said aloud. Now he'll think I'm pathetic and weak, she thought. And then she thought, I *am* pathetic and weak. If he hadn't called before I could have made up reasons to excuse it. He got in too late, or was on punishment and couldn't call, or his mother or sister was on the phone until late. Now if he doesn't call I have to worry that he knew I'd called and just didn't want to be bothered. Shoot, I shouldn't have called. Or I could have at least not left my name.

When Jillian came home fifteen minutes later Kylie chatted with her for a few minutes then went up to her room to do some homework. A half hour into her studies the telephone rang and she held her breath as she waited to see if Jillian would call up, "Kylie, telephone." But the yell never came and she went back to her homework. Twenty minutes later the telephone rang again, and this time Jillian did call her.

"Hello," Kylie said.

"What's up?" Ian said.

"You tell me," Kylie said before she even thought. She nearly slapped herself on the forehead for being so stupid. She had planned to play it cool, to almost ignore what had happened in the hallway unless he brought it up.

"Whatcha mean?"

"Nothing."

"It doesn't sound like nothing," he said.

"Well, it is," Kylie said, trying, but not quite succeeding, in changing her voice so that she didn't sound bothered.

"Tell me," Ian urged. His voice was so unexpectedly gentle that Kylie relented and told the truth.

"Why did you blow me off today in the hallway?"

"I didn't blow you off, Kylie."

"Yes, you did, Ian."

"Well, I didn't mean to. I was just hanging with my friends, you know, chillin', that's all. I thought you might hang around or something," he added lamely.

"I didn't know anybody over there but you, and you acted as if you didn't know me at all. You hardly looked at me."

Damn, Ian thought. "I'm sorry, okay?"

"Why did you act that way?"

"First of all, I think you're overreacting. And secondly, I am sorry, 'cause I didn't mean for it to come across like that at all."

"All right," Kylie said almost grudgingly.

"Really?"

"Really. I guess I shouldn't have made such a big deal about it," Kylie said, ignoring the small voice inside her that told her to ask again, and get a real answer.

Kylie and Ian sat on a bench in a park not far from Kylie's home watching as the sun set. It was two days since Ian's cold shoulder in the hallway. The temperature was an unexpectedly mild forty-three degrees and they were bundled in warm jackets with their hands shoved into their pockets. They had been outside, talking intimately for nearly an hour. Ian was surprised at how easy it was to talk to her.

She'd just finished telling him a funny story about Nae Nae and Stevie when he said, "You never mention your father."

"There's nothing to mention. He got my mother pregnant, was around for a hot second when I was a baby, and then, poof . . . he was gone."

"You never see him?"

"Oh, once in a while. I guess he'll develop some temporary case of conscience and then call or pop over. I saw him three times last year, and twice this year. Typical, for him."

"Damn, that's messed up."

"Once I tried to get my father to come for me," she said.

"Yeah?"

She could feel his eyes on the side of her face, but his gaze did not embarrass her. "Yeah. I wrote him letters when I was nine. I thought that if I told him everything about me he would want to see me, want to be with me. So I told him about my new gym shoes, an 'A' that I'd gotten on a spelling test, how the art teacher had picked me as supply captain two weeks in a row, and how I'd gotten two certificates that year. One for perfect attendance and the other one for citizenship." She looked over at Ian then and he was looking at her steadily, his eyes intent. I drew him three pictures, I forget what the other two were, but one of them was the two of us, standing in front of a tree, holding hands. I sent one or two letters out every week for almost a month."

"What happened?" he asked, his voice low and tender, like a hand on her back.

"They all came back."

"All of them?"

"Every single one. In one envelope, all unopened. He'd moved and the lady he'd been staying with wrote and told me that she'd held on to them in case he called. But he didn't, and she didn't know where he was, she wrote me, so she'd sent them back to me."

"Damn," Ian said.

"Yeah. She wrote me on this little sheet of stationery with tiny pink and yellow flowers all around the edge and her handwriting was pretty. I remember thinking that because of that, the paper and the handwriting, she must be nice. But he left her anyway."

They were quiet for a while after that.

"Do you ever worry that you'll never amount to much?" Ian asked her as he looked ahead at the sky.

"Yes, doesn't everybody?"

"I don't know." Overhead a flock of birds glided by in their intuitive arrow, pointing south, kissing heaven, not looking back but holding the code to return again and again. Kylie watched them, her head tilted back slightly. Ian followed her glance for a few moments and then continued his study of the setting sun. "Sometimes I think about the fact that so many of the grown-ups I know don't get it right."

"What's 'it'?" Kylie asked.

"Life, I guess. Relationships, whatever, fill in the blank. If the people responsible for teaching us don't have it right, how are we ever supposed to do it?"

"I never thought of it that way."

"I wish that I never had. The blind leading the blind," he said in quiet disgust. "I want to do something important with my life . . . but I have no idea what. Isn't that hopeless?"

"No, not really. It's just being young, I think. I think a lot of people feel like that when they're our age."

"You do something important." He turned to look at her. "You take good care of your brother and sister. You really help your mother, you're . . ."

"Like a mother myself," she finished for him. "That's not my big goal in life."

"No, but at least you already know that you can do something that matters, that you can stick to it. That counts for a lot."

"Yeah, right." She was gently sarcastic.

"No, I'm not kidding, Kylie. I respect that about you, it's cool."

"Thanks," she said as she turned to him. "When you came over my house that time and stayed for the dinner that I cooked . . . I felt like an old woman. Cooking the meal, minding the kids, and all that."

"No, not old." He kissed her on the lips then. "Sweet."

Chapter 11

"No!" Kylie laughed, her voice dangerously near a screech. "Stop, Ian, I mean it." She stood precariously upon a pair of rented ice skates. It was after one on Saturday afternoon and the sky was pale blue, clear and vast, holding the distant sun like a weakened torch. Ian spun easily around her, taunting her by pretending that he was going to topple her. They'd strolled through Detroit's historic Greektown, going into some of the jewelry, clothing, and trinket shops. Then they'd continued wandering downtown and eventually ended up at the Campus Martius ice skating rink.

"You can't skate," he said as he laughed at her.

"I told you that, Sherlock!"

"I know, I know. But I had to see it for myself to really

believe it." He was circling her like a beautiful vulture as he spoke.

"Stop that," she ordered, "you're making me dizzy."

He grabbed her by the waist as he stopped in front of her. She began to wobble violently as she looked into his laughing eyes. He moved easily and pulled her tightly against him, allowing his balance to stabilize her. "You're okay," he said softly, "don't worry, I've got you."

Kylie stopped laughing as she looked at him. "I know," she said.

"You know," Ian said softly as he held her close, "most people who can roller-skate are fine when they get on ice skates. That's why I asked if you could roller-skate before I brought you here."

"I guess I'm not most people," Kylie answered softly.

"I guess not." He kissed her after he said that and he closed his eyes in order to absorb her all the better. Last night he had gone to a party at Michael's hosted by the members of FBI and the pledges. Tricia and her girls were there. The party had been too sweet. Michael's parents were away for the weekend and his twenty-three-year-old brother Matthew was in charge of making sure Michael didn't tear up the house or draw police attention. Matthew was former FBI, so he knew what to expect and how to keep things in check while still letting them have a good time. The music was bouncing, the girls were hot, there was plenty to drink, and while the upstairs was off-limits the basement had two guest bedrooms. Their indoor pool was crowded with hot girls in tiny bikinis, and bare-chested guys in baggy swim trunks. Michael's parents had decorated early for Christmas, and lights inside and outside of the pool's room illuminated the freshly fallen snow that could be seen outside of the partially frosted glass walls.

Ian had called Kylie before he left for the party and invited her to go ice-skating with him today. With that all set he felt that he could go ahead and enjoy his night, and that's just what he did. He had had a great time: everybody seemed to know who he was. The music was off the hook, the girls were fine and many of them were so wild. It was just the way that he had imagined parties would be for him when he became a part of FBI.

At one point during the party, he'd found himself standing near Jason Vincent, the star point guard of Crosses' varsity basketball team. They were in the same grade and had become cool with one another while taking the same tenth-grade biology class. "What's up, man?" Ian said as he gave Jason a play.

"Oh, hey Ian, what's up?" Jason said as he struggled to tear his eyes away from something across the room. Ian followed Jason's gaze and saw the girl that he'd heard Jason dumped his girlfriend Lisa for. She was cute, Ian thought, but Lisa was gorgeous and sexy, and for the first time, Ian saw a relationship between what Jason had gone through and what he was experiencing with Kylie. There had definitely been talk when Jason broke up with Lisa and started going with this new girl, but Jason hadn't seemed to care. But, Ian thought, Jason could probably afford to handle his business like that because of the way that he moved the basketball on the court. Ian didn't have that going for him. All of a sudden Ian really wanted to ask Jason how he'd had the courage to do it, to break away from what everybody he hung with said he ought to want, and go for what he *really* wanted. But what do I really want, Ian wondered.

"That's your girl, huh?" Ian asked.

Jason glanced at Ian before looking back across the room. "Yeah, that's her, Kyra." Ian caught the warmth in his voice and pushed back an unexpected pang of jealousy. He looked at Kyra sitting on a love seat with two other girls. She was wedged in on the end of the seat, obviously uncomfortable and not looking thrilled to be there. "She's ready to go," Jason said with a smile to Ian. "She told me that she didn't want to come, but I just wanted to stop through for a minute, you know, check it out."

"Yeah," Ian said.

"We're gonna bounce, though, man," Jason said as he gave Ian another play.

"You ain't been here no time, you gonna let her make you go?" Ian asked.

"Naw, it's not like that. I'd rather go if she's not feelin' it. It's better when it's just the two of us anyway." And Ian knew that Jason wasn't just talking about messing around with her, but that he meant being with her. A few minutes later he watched as the couple left, Jason's arm loose around his girl's shoulders, neither of them looking back.

He had thought of Kylie off and on during the rest of the party and he awoke this morning really looking forward to seeing her.

A couple of families were on the ice along with an old couple dressed in matching red, white, and blue Bavarian-style sweaters. A young couple who really knew what they were doing were gliding easily and beautifully by.

"Are you cold?" he asked her.

"A little."

"Ready to go?"

"Not yet. Take me around the rink one more time, okay?"

"Okay," Ian said. He took her gloved hands in his and began skating backward, gently tugging her along. "Bend your knees some. And pick up your feet when you feel like you can."

"All right," Kylie said as she kept her eyes on the ice and their feet. "Why are you so good at this?"

"I've been skating since I was a little kid. My mama used to love to take my sister and me to Hart Plaza on the weekends." Hart Plaza's ice-skating rink was near the Detroit River.

"Really? You just don't hear about a lot of black ice-skaters," she said.

"Well, I guess the number rises by one today, thanks to you."

Kylie looked up then and smiled at Ian. They had rounded the skating rink by now. "I don't think anyone else would call this skating."

"You're right. Come on, you deserve a treat for trying so hard."

They left the skating rink and went to Union Street, a restaurant only five minutes away near Wayne State

University's campus. They each had thick corned-beef sandwiches, clam chowder, and hot chocolate.

"Ian, this food is so good."

"Yeah, it's tight. I always get full when I eat here."

Kylie lifted one half of her huge sandwich. "I can see why!"

"So how are Nae Nae and Stevie doing?"

"Oh, they're fine. They're starting to bug me to death because I promised to take them to the Festival of Lights next weekend, and they just cannot wait."

"Aw, man, I haven't been to that since I was real little," Ian exclaimed. Kylie loved the way the glints of gold in his hazel eyes danced when he got excited.

"Is that right?"

"Yeah. My pops used to pack us all up in the car and drive us down there to check it out. I loved it when I was a kid. All those pretty lights, and the trees were amazing, like something out of a book or movie."

The Festival of Lights was a lovely display of beautifully decorated Christmas trees, from dwarf pines to enormous Norwegian spruce, held inside of Detroit's downtown convention center.

"You should come with us," Kylie said impulsively.

"No . . . no, your mother wouldn't want me tagging along."

"She's not coming. We got some free tickets from a neighbor, but my mother has to work overtime that night. She's going to come and pick us up and take us during her dinner break."

"Well, then, yeah, I want to come. I could drive us, if you like."

"That would be cool." She watched across the table for a moment. "It sounds like your father had his good points," Kylie said thoughtfully.

"He did . . . he still does. He just doesn't have a lot of time. At least not for my sister and me."

"Maybe you could call and invite him to do some things."

"I did at first. But he would cancel, or act like he couldn't take his eyes off his watch or whatever. He stood us up a few times, too."

"That's messed up."

"Yeah, it was. So I rarely try to hook up with him. My sister said if he wanted to see us, he would. I invited him to the talent show, though. He said he might come. My half sister has a recital the same night, so we'll see."

Kylie looked across the table at Ian and without thinking stretched her hand across the table and placed it atop his warm, brown hand. She didn't say anything because she didn't know what to say. She knew exactly how it felt to have a father who behaved like an ass sometimes: irresponsible, thoughtless, and childish. She understood the hurt it caused and hated to think of Ian experiencing it. Ian turned his hand over gently so that he could hold Kylie's hand in the palm of his. He squeezed her hand softly and released it.

"It's no big deal, for real. It used to really bother me when I was younger, but I'm mostly used to it now," Ian said. He gave her a half smile.

Kylie returned the half smile. "Okay."

"Is that how you feel about your father?"

"I'm like you, it bothered me a lot when I was little, but it's not so bad anymore."

"I guess it's pretty bad for Stevie and Nae Nae."

"No, we don't have the same father. Their dad comes around a lot. He's cool."

"That's good. How does he treat you?"

"Me? Oh, Larry is all right with me. He doesn't try to be my father or anything. But he's cool. He gives me money on my birthday, and a gift when he brings Christmas presents over for Nae Nae and Stevie. He always asks me how I'm doing in school and whatnot. He's fine."

"That's good." Ian leaned back in his seat, taking a breather after finishing his meal. Kylie was only picking over what was left on her plate. She looked up at him and he was struck again by how honest and open her look was: she liked him, very much. The thought didn't make him feel all cocky, instead he felt . . . good, even a little humbled. Impulsively, he told her, "I want to own my own architecture firm when I grow up, do some projects that improve Detroit."

"Really?"

"Yeah. I have a lot of ideas. I blow off some of my classes, but never drafting." He looked across at her to find her listening and caring about what he said. "Anyway, I don't know."

"I'd like to see some of your drawings sometime," Kylie said.

"I'd like to show you." But he needed to change the subject because he didn't plan to be with her long enough to show her any drawings, and the guilt that that thought gave him sliced across his good mood. "You almost ready?"

"Yeah, I'm done."

"Let's go over my house for a while."

"All right."

Once they were at Ian's place, Ian unlocked the door and they were greeted by loud R & B music and a young woman's wailing voice. "That's my sister," Ian said. "She can*not* sing!" Kylie smiled and following Ian's lead, took off her wet boots before they left the foyer.

This was Kylie's first time at Ian's house, and she tried to get a look around as she followed him. It was a comfortable-looking place with mostly black and beige furniture and neat piles of magazines, books, and newspapers scattered around. There were pictures of a younger Ian and a little girl, but Kylie didn't get a chance to get a good look at them before they hit the kitchen.

"What's up?" Ian greeted the young woman sitting at the table watching music videos on a small color television. Slender, with short sandy hair and golden skin, Ian's sister looked back at Kylie with the same hazel eyes Ian had.

"What's up?" she said back.

"Kim, this is Kylie; Kylie, this is my sister, Kim."

"Hi," both said.

"We're gonna be upstairs," Ian informed his sister.

"All right," she said giving Kylie a look over. "But, don't be up there all day, Ian."

"Whatever," Ian answered casually as he turned and left the room with Kylie right behind him.

This whole "we'll be upstairs" thing was news to Kylie and her heartbeat quickened and sweat formed in the palms of her hands.

"Where's your mother?" Kylie asked as they went up the stairs.

"She's at work. Why are you whispering?"

She hadn't even realized that she was whispering. "When is she supposed to come home?"

"She probably won't be back until eleven tonight or something. Don't worry, everything is okay." Kylie didn't answer and despite Ian's easy tone her heartbeat didn't slow down a bit.

Done in blues, tans, and browns, Ian's room was pleasant and, surprisingly, neat. He had posters of sexy female singers and actresses on his walls. He had a desk and chair in warm brown wood. Above the desk were two wooden shelves upon which sat a small CD player/radio set and some books and magazines. There was a tall dresser, and a full-size bed in the same dark wood. The bed was pushed against one wall and the navy comforter was neatly made up.

Ian took off his coat and eased Kylie out of hers. He placed both coats on his chair then plopped down across the width of his bed. "Come here," he said, extending his hand to her. She took it, trying hard not to show her nervousness, and sat beside him on the bed. Her pink-socked feet looked small next to his large ones. "Why do you look so scared, girl? I'm not going to bite you," he said softly.

"No?"

"Naw, I'm gonna kiss you right here," he said as he kissed her left cheek. "And here," he whispered before kissing her right cheek. "Can I kiss you here?" he asked as he touched her forehead gently with his index finger. Kylie nodded, unable to say anything. Ian laughed softly. "Are my kisses that good, or that bad?"

At that moment, Kylie felt intoxicated, transported, and electric, all at once. To have him so close, speaking to her so gently, with the two of them tucked away in this room alone was more than she could have ever imagined. It was more, and better and sweeter. She wanted it to go on forever, never stopping, never changing. She leaned in toward Ian and caught his lips beneath hers. The tenderness of his lips was singing out to her and made her want more, and she kissed him as though she were caught in a dream, opening her mouth over his as she felt his lips opening to her. The kiss pulled itself along, and in it she could hear Ian telling her how much he liked her.

When they parted from that kiss they immediately fell into the next kiss, and the next, and the next, and Kylie could not say when they went from sitting to lying side by side. They just were suddenly. While her hands were wrapped tenderly around his neck, Ian's hands seemed to be absolutely everywhere: her breasts, thighs, and for a while at the warmth at the top of her thighs, then her stomach and neck. He had her so aroused that she could barely breathe.

"Ian, wait, please."

"No, I don't want to, and you don't want to either," he murmured without stilling his hands for a moment.

"Yes, I do, Ian." Kylie pushed against his chest to force them apart. "I want to stop."

"Okay, okay, we'll stop." He pulled away and propped himself up on one elbow and looked down on her. "What's the matter?"

"I don't know, it's too fast."

"You've never had sex, have you?" he whispered.

"No, never."

"Not any kind of sex?"

"No, just touching, like we do. But not as much as us. This is too fast." She took deep breaths trying to slow down the beating of her heart.

"No it's not, baby. Not if we both enjoy it. It's a real natural thing to do." He kissed her neck gently, then pulled back and watched her again. She could see the arousal in his eyes; they had taken on a darker hue, almost a warm brown color. "What if I just stay up here, above the waist?" His grin was positively wicked. "Hmm? That should be all right, shouldn't it?"

"Okay," Kylie said. She smiled at him despite herself. "Just above the waist," she echoed.

"That's right." He perched above her on his elbow as he began kissing her on the mouth again. He allowed his lips to create a trail to her neck, slowly lace her neck with delicate kisses, then caress her collarbone. All the while his hand cupped her breast, rubbing it gently.

Ian lost himself in the feel of her, her gentle willingness urging him on. He tried to make himself remember that he was running a game, but it didn't feel like it to him, not at this moment. Oh, Kylie, I like you, I really do, he thought.

"Oh, Kylie." Ian held his breath for a moment, he hadn't meant to say that out loud. Damn! Damn, damn, damn! Much to his relief Kylie didn't say anything, and before she could he placed his mouth atop hers for another kiss. He slipped his hand underneath her sweater and felt the smooth texture of her bra and at the same time felt her stiffen beneath his hand. Go slow, he cautioned himself silently. So that's what he did—instead of trying to get her bra off, which he badly wanted to do, he just caressed the outside of her bra. The more he did it, the more intense her kisses became, and he realized, so did his. He wanted her so badly now. He didn't just want her for the bet, either, but because he desired *her*.

He reminded himself to take it slow and not frighten her. He had time . . . not a lot, though.

Later that night, Ian and Michael occupied a booth near the door in The Biz. They nursed sodas and waited for their friends to show up. No one had put any money in the jukebox and the place wasn't crowded, so when the door opened to incoming customers, Ian could hear the slushing, slooshing sound of the snow under passing tires.

"So what's up with you and that girl?" Michael asked.

"What, from the dance?" Ian asked.

"Yeah. What's her name?"

"Kylie. Nothing, you know. We're talking, I've taken her out a couple of times, we've done some messing around." Ian toyed with a straw wrapped in paper as he spoke. He did not look up at Mike.

"So, you gonna be able to hit that by the deadline?"

"That's the plan," Ian stripped the paper slowly from the straw. "That's the plan," he said, nearly to himself.

"So how is she so far?" Mike asked.

"Why are you so curious?" Ian said as he looked Mike, finally, in the eyes.

Mike shrugged. "Just wondering man. I do have a hundred bills riding on it, you know."

"Forget the money," Ian said. "I'll just do it as my last challenge and let that be that."

Mike looked at him for a while after that. Ian couldn't tell what he was thinking. "Why are turning down the chance to win a hundred bills?"

"Taking a hundred dollars for sleeping with her, it just doesn't feel right, man, that's all. So forget the money."

"Whatever you say, Ian." Mike was still looking at Ian so intently that Ian looked away again.

"What's up?" Mike called. Ian turned around to see the rest of FBI walk through the door. Their presence filled up the space where he and Mike's conversation had been, and Ian was glad. The less he talked about Kylie, the better.

Chapter 12

Sunday afternoon moved tranquilly as Kylie sat ironing Nae Nae's and Stevie's clothes for the coming school week. She listened to music as she worked and dreamed of Ian. She recalled yesterday, which was so delicious she couldn't help but smile every time she thought of it. Then she pictured a future of going places with him, hanging with him in the hallway, and standing outside in the students' parking lot leaning against his car. She saw stolen kisses in the hallway between classes, trips back out to the coffeehouse, and parking out at Belle Isle.

Yesterday, he'd dropped her off around 4 P.M. and had called her at 5 P.M. She didn't really know how far she planned to go with Ian, she didn't even want to think about it. She only knew that she wanted to be with him.

Fully considering how far she might go seemed to weigh down the sweetness of what she and Ian did. She loved things the way that they were now. Kylie knew about a couple of girls her age who had sex, but she didn't know them well enough to be in their business. Tracy, Desiree, and she were all virgins, and they had no plans to change that in the near future. They figured sex carried too much baggage with it, they could wait. In the past Kylie had never known a boy with whom she would have even considered having sex. She had messed around with a boy named Tony last spring and summer in a romance that had never jelled into going together. Neither of them had felt the urge to take the relationship or the messing-around to the next level.

But now, with Ian, she felt the tug to go farther and faster and she felt more and more willing to say yes. And that frightened her some, because then what? She didn't know.

Whenever Jillian spoke to her about sex she told Kylie to wait, but that if she did decide to do it, to be sure to use protection. Kylie recalled two years ago when Jillian had sat her down at the table and spelled it all out for her. "You don't want to get pregnant or get a disease, girl," Jillian had said as she looked across the table at Kylie. "I don't really want you to have sex when you're so young. It's too complicated. But at the same time, I'm not stupid. I know some kids do it. You've got to use a condom one-hundred-percent of the time. And if you're messin' with a boy who can't respect that, there's no point spending five more minutes on him, 'cause he doesn't give a damn about you, and that's the truth. He's just as well as told you he'd rather have your sex than your life. You see what I'm sayin'?"

Kylie nodded mutely, taking in everything that her mother said. Although Jillian wasn't terribly affectionate, Kylie knew she loved her children very much.

"Now, you can tell me if you're having sex. I'm not gonna like it, but I'll answer every question you got if I know the answer, and I'll go with you to get some contraception. You don't want to get pregnant, AIDS, or any other STD. So we'll find you something. Okay?"

Kylie nodded again.

"Now, there's only one way to guarantee that you won't get pregnant or sick, and that's to not have sex. That's the best way. So you think about everything I'm saying. And you especially think about it when some boy is whispering sweet nothin's in your ear and you can hardly think straight. You pull yourself together enough to think about what your mama said, and take care of yourself, Kylie."

Since that time, Jillian would remind Kylie of different points from her speech, and Kylie took her mother's words seriously. She wasn't sexually active and she had never had any intention of being so before. But now, with Ian in her life, she wasn't sure what direction she would take. However, she did know that she would follow her mother's advice, and use a condom at all times.

But anyway, she reminded herself, it wasn't even at that point, yet. It might never get there. Ian wasn't even her *boyfriend.* She didn't plan to have sex with someone who wasn't at least hers.

She was finished with the children's clothes now, and she could smell Jillian's beef stew simmering upstairs. Nae Nae and Stevie were occupied building a town out of Legos.

"Kylie, telephone," Jillian called.

"I've got it," Kylie spoke into the receiver. "Hello?"

"What's up, Kylie?"

"Hey, Ian. What's up with you?"

"Nothing, you know. Just callin' to check you out."

"Cool."

"So, you wanna go to that café again this Friday?"

"Yeah, sure. I have to watch the kids Friday night, though."

"Well, we could go in the early evening if you want, or if you can."

"I'd like that."

"And I was thinking, after the Festival of Lights on Saturday, why don't we come over my house? My mom is working late."

"But my mother will be at work, too."

"What time does she get off?"

"Um, eight-thirty."

"What time does she usually get home?"

"Before nine."

"Oh, well that's cool. Just ask your mom if we can hang out after we bring the kids home. If she says yes, you can come over my house."

Kylie blushed. "Okay, I'll ask."

"Bet. We'll take the kids for pizza or something until your mom's home."

"All right." She couldn't believe how much he wanted to spend time with her. For the rest of the conversation Kylie floated on a small cloud of happiness.

Chapter 13

"So we're set for tonight?" Ian asked.

"Yeah, we're set. You have to come inside when you come over, though; my mama won't let me go anywhere with you if you don't."

"That's cool. I'll be by at nine-thirty, right?"

"Right," Tricia said.

For Ian, Friday had arrived quickly between calling Kylie, flirting with Tricia, and hanging out with his boys. Tonight there was a party at the Cradle on East Jefferson. The place was sure to be hoppin', and Ian had asked Tricia if she wanted to go with him. He hadn't really expected her to say yes since girls loved to go out in groups, but she'd surprised him. Now that they had all the details sorted out he had only one real problem. He was all set to go out with Kylie that same evening.

"Here comes your girlfriend, Ian," Tricia said in a teasing voice. Mike, Dante, Zaire, and a few other kids laughed.

Ian looked down the hall only to see Kylie walking his way with one of her friends. Great, he thought, just perfect. He wanted to hide, he wanted to melt away like snow in spring and return again when the weather was more . . . suitable. "Yeah, whatever," he mumbled in response to Tricia.

"What's up, Ian?" Kylie called when she neared the group.

"What's up?" Ian called. He didn't move, though he knew he should have.

Kylie's friend looked at Ian, her eyes hard and cold, reading the situation perfectly. Ian turned his eyes away from her, glanced around, and found himself looking into Kylie's midnight eyes. Do something, he told himself. But what? If he went over to her in front of all of his friends they might bother him about it, but if he just ignored her again . . . damn. He stepped away from Tricia and his clique and went over to Kylie. Kylie had already taken a few steps toward him and away from her friend.

Kylie looked at him with slightly suspicious eyes. "Hey, Ian."

"What's up, girl?" he said softly. He was glad to see her, he just didn't want to see her *here*.

"You still comin' over at five?"

"Yeah, I'll be there."

"Okay," she said, still standing stock still. Waiting.

But Ian knew that he wasn't going to walk her anywhere. He had to get rid of her. Now, but nicely, if he could. "So, I'll see you later, okay?" he said, and started backing away from her. Guilt stiffened his stride, and he kept his eyes away from Tricia as he walked away from Kylie.

"All right." She glanced at the crowd behind Ian, looked at Ian again, and then headed over to her friend. Ian watched as they walked away.

"So, Ian, is your girl gonna start coming by on the regular, or what?" Mike asked.

"She's not my girl."

"Whatever you say, man." Mike laughed.

"Look, Ian," Tricia said, "I don't want to get in you-all's way, or anything." She started laughing and her friends joined in.

"Funny," Ian said as he took her by her waist and tickled her lightly. She folded into him easily, and he held her like that for a few moments before letting her go.

He knew that if Tricia showed up when he was with his boys he would gladly pull her on over for all the other boys to admire. But the thought of claiming Kylie in front of his friends still embarrassed him.

He had to wrap this challenge up before the weekend was over. He had it all planned out. After the Festival of Lights his mother wouldn't be home because she had a date, and Kim was going on a weekend trip to Chicago with a couple of her girlfriends. He'd have the place all to himself that evening. He'd bring Kylie back and have sex with her then. But first he'd have to spend some time with her tonight. He had to at least get her to take her top off, or it might be too hard to get her to go all the way the next night.

For some reason, despite himself, he kept thinking of the phrase his ninth-grade teacher had used as they studied some book called *Of Mice and Men*. She'd said something like, "the best laid schemes of mice and men . . ." But for the life of him he couldn't remember how the quote ended. All he seemed to remember was that in the book, the plans didn't end well at all.

When the school day ended for Ian, he was still thinking of Kylie and the way that he'd blown her off earlier in the day. He decided to stop by her locker for a few minutes before he headed out. Besides, he wanted to see her. He rounded the corner to the hallway where her locker was and saw her there talking to some boy. Of course Ian had seen him before, but he didn't know his name. Whatever his name, he was all into Kylie, that was obvious.

"What's up?" Ian said when he got to them.

Kylie ignored him and finished her response to Terrance. Terrance glanced at Ian and back at Kylie.

"Oh, hi, Ian," Kylie said.

"What's up?" the other guy said.

"You two know each other?" Kylie asked. They both shook their heads no.

"Ian, this is Terrance, Terrance, Ian."

The two nodded to one another.

"So, I'll talk to you later, okay, Terrance?"

"That's cool. I'll call you tonight."

"All right, see you later."

"Later," Terrance said and walked off.

"So," Ian said after Terrance left.

"So."

"So, I'm looking forward to going out with you tonight."

"Yeah, but you're not looking forward to seeing me in front of your friends."

"What? Didn't I come over to you?"

"Yeah, but . . ."

"But what? I don't want everyone knowing all my business. Is that so bad?" He leaned in close. "Hmm?"

"I guess not."

"You guess not?" he said, kissing one cheek.

"I guess."

"Are you gonna be nice to me tonight, or are you gonna act all mean?"

She looked into his eyes and smiled so sweetly he felt it inside himself. "I'll be nice to you," she said.

"I can't wait to get my hands on you, you know that?"

Kylie laughed.

"So who is this Terrance?"

"A friend of mine. He's in my algebra class. He's tutoring me."

"Yeah? It looks like he's diggin' on you. Looks like he wants to tutor you in more than math."

"Whatever, Ian," Kylie said.

"Okay, girl," he said as he squeezed her waist. "See you at five. I won't be late." He kissed her cheek again and left.

"What's up, Mr. Hill?" Ian had been waiting five minutes to have a word with his counselor. Mr. Hill was, as usual, well-dressed in a professional yet understated way. Ian had once commented on how sweet his shoes always were, and Mr. Hill had said, "Ah, well, thank you, Mr. Striver. Take my advice: always take good care of your feet and your feet will always take good care of you. If your feet are ailing you, it will be very hard to focus on anything else." Ian had just chuckled and shook his head. You never knew exactly where Mr. Hill might take you when you entered a conversation with him, but 9.5 times out of ten, he ended up telling you something that you could use right then or later.

Today he looked even busier than usual.

"Ian, good to see you. Have a seat." Mr. Hill shut the file drawer he had been looking in and sat down at his desk.

"Pretty busy, huh?"

"The usual. What do you need today?"

"Nothing . . . really."

"Well, I've got a little of that. Anything else?" he asked with a smile.

"At my age, which do you think is more important, finding a good romance or good friendships?"

"I'd have to say friendships, if I had to pick one. Are you getting romantically serious about someone?"

"Something like that."

"Do you want to talk about it?"

"Naw. Nothing like that." Ian smiled and started

rising from his seat. "I'll stop by before too long. Take it easy."

"Ian, just a moment. I'll tell you this, though you didn't ask," Mr. Hill said smiling. "Being a good friend and a good boyfriend take some of the same qualities. You should treat the young woman you're with *at least* as well as you'd treat a good friend."

"Thanks, Mr. Hill," Ian said, already back in motion.

Mr. Hill nodded slowly and said, "Oh, Ian."

"Yes."

"I heard you're pledging FBI."

"FBI?" Ian said, as he stepped back over to Mr. Hill's desk. "Sorry, never heard of it." No FBI member or pledge was allowed to speak of their fraternity with any adult.

"Right," Mr. Hill said, looking through Ian like freshly cleaned glass. "Nonetheless, you be careful there. I *have* heard of them, and I'll tell you this—when you let a group's identity define you, you can lose who you are. That's never good."

Ian threw on one of his charming smiles and said, "Thanks for the pearls of wisdom, Mr. Hill, but like I said, I've never heard of FBI, other than the federal agency, that is."

"Well, come by whenever you need."

"Okay." As Ian walked down the hall he wished he'd had the nerve to open up and be honest with Mr. Hill about the challenge and Kylie. But right now he had neither the time nor the inclination. He checked his watch. He had to be at Kylie's in less than two hours, and he didn't want to be late.

In fact, he was ten minutes early when he pulled up outside Kylie's place. They left right away, and everything went just as Ian had planned. Their time at the coffeehouse was excellent again. They talked, laughed, and enjoyed the food and music. She came back to his house just as he wanted, and with soft music whispering around them they kissed and messed around until both of them were topless, breathless, and caught up in the excitement.

"Ian," Kylie whispered as his hand left her breast and headed quickly and deliberately for the button on her jeans. He ignored her, undid the button, and unzipped the zipper. His hand was inside her pants before she could catch her breath.

"Kylie, you're driving me crazy, girl," he whispered into her neck. "I want you so badly. When are you gonna let me make love to you, Kylie?"

"I don't know, I don't know if we should."

"Why shouldn't we?" he whispered.

"Because," she said. He listened to her quick breathing as he felt the warmth of her and thought that he was, in fact, a little crazy about her.

"No 'because,' Kylie, no 'because.' You know I like you, so much. I'll use a condom. And baby, it'll feel so good. So good. Even better than what we're doing right now."

She moaned softly.

"Can I make love to you tomorrow?"

"I don't know," she said, her voice straining with the conflict. "I can't think."

"Don't then, don't think all the time. Sometimes you have to go with what you feel." He kissed her mouth for a long, tender time. "Just tell me what you feel, not what you think."

"I want to," she said.

"Yes, that's it." And he only felt a little a guilty as he continued, his hands all over her and his mind a tangle of lust, longing, and the guilt of his insincerity.

"Desiree?" Kylie said into the telephone later that night.

"Yeah. Kylie?"

"Yeah." Kylie paused for a moment, thinking, wondering how to ask her question. "How do you know if you're in love?"

"I don't know. I really don't, never been there. Why?"

"I don't know."

"Do you think you're in love with Ian, Kylie?"

"I think. But I don't know."

"If I tell you something do you promise that you won't get mad?"

"Yes."

"I don't trust him, Kylie. He's a player and a hater. You remember last year when it got all around that he slept with those two girls?"

"Yeah."

"Well, I heard that it got all around because *he* did the tellin'."

Kylie's response was a thoughtful, anxious silence.

"Just be careful, Kylie. What's to stop him from taking

your business and spreading it all over the street? And there's no reason to believe that he thinks he's in love, too. He could be planning to use you, just like he used those other girls."

"But if you could only see the way he treats me."

"Like how?" Kylie told Desiree about all of the places Ian and she had been and the way he treated her when they were alone. "That sounds good, girl, for real. But how do we know that he wasn't just as good to those other girls?"

"You're right, but Desiree, when I'm with him all I can think about is how good he makes me feel! And I can't get enough of it, Dez. It doesn't seem like he's playing me."

"I hope you're right." Dez thought a moment before she asked her next question. "So are you thinking about having sex with him or something?"

"Well . . . we've already done a lot of 'or something.'"

"Like what, girl?" Kylie could hear the excitement in her friend's voice.

"Kissing, of course, and touching . . . down there . . ."

"You touched him, too?" Desiree interrupted.

"Yeah, a little. I let him undo my shirt, we messed around on his bed, you know, lying down together."

"Dang, Kylie, you've been movin' right along, girl!"

"I know. I wanted to tell you and Tracy, but it just all felt so new. I had to kind of think about it by myself for a while."

"I understand. But look, Kylie, be careful. Look out for yourself." Dez paused for only a beat before she said, "You're really thinking about doing it with him, aren't you?"

"I don't know. Maybe I am thinking about it."

"Has he tried?"

"You know he has."

"What did you tell him?" Dez said.

"I said maybe."

"Maybe? Not 'no.'"

"Not no. And I told him that I wanted to."

"Girl, you're crazy. Don't do it with him. You just got with that boy!"

"I know, but I think I love him, you know? And who am I going to do it with if I don't do it with somebody I love."

"But you should wait."

"Until when? Until I'm married?" Kylie asked. "Are you going to wait until you're married?"

"I don't know. My mama said I'd *better* wait until then."

"Well, I always thought that I'd wait until I was in love. But I figured that I would fall in love when I was older, but now . . ."

"But now you shouldn't commit to anything," Dez said.

Kylie laughed. "Well, all I said was maybe."

"Kylie, don't even think about doing it without a condom."

"I won't."

"And really think before you do have sex, if you do. Think about if it's what you want to do, or if you're just doing it to keep Ian interested. Because, once you lose it, you can't get your virginity back. Ever."

"I hear you."

Kylie got off the telephone with her friend's last words echoing in her mind. She went to her room and shut the door and lay down in the dark thinking. She was scared and excited when she thought about being with Ian. She knew that a big part of her felt that having sex with Ian would keep him close, and having him close would fill that space where loneliness sometimes sat. She wished that she could be sure, sure that if she said "no" he would be there anyway, or if she said "yes" that he would stay.

But there was no way of knowing, not without asking. And she could not make herself ask.

Chapter 14

Kylie spent all of Saturday morning and afternoon in a fog. No boy had ever made her feel the way that Ian had. No one had ever touched her that way, kissed her that way, spoken to her that way. If he had kept going, she was pretty sure that she would have had sex with him last night. He had made her feel so good, so lost and so found at the same time, that just thinking of them together made her face flood with heat and her stomach tight. In fact, she wasn't quite sure, but she thought that she may have agreed to have sex with him already. His hands had been so good, his lips so soft and hot, that she couldn't be quite sure what she'd said or agreed to do.

Now Nae Nae, Stevie, Ian, and she were walking through Cobo Hall together headed to the Festival of Lights exhibit, and she felt like she was walking on a cloud. Ian was so nice to her sister and brother, when either of them said something silly she and Ian would look at one another and there was this clear understanding between them "these kids, so cute," their eyes seemed to communicate.

When they got to the door of the exhibit, Kylie handed the lady their tickets and Stevie shot off for the first tree. It stood about seven feet tall, a handsome fir decorated in gold and red. The lights twinkled, the ornamental balls shone, and ornaments of expertly crafted fairy creatures hung from branches. "Oh man, look at this," Stevie squeaked.

"Slow down," Kylie called.

"I got him," Ian said and went to stand beside Stevie. "Aw yeah, that's sweet, little man," Ian told him. Stevie looked up at Ian and smiled. Kylie and Nae Nae joined them inside the exhibit room.

"Look at this one," Nae Nae called after they had admired the first tree for a bit. She stood before a miniature that sat upon a table. It was done up with soft pink-and-fern-colored ornaments and antique silver decorations. Brown and pink ballerinas leaped, pointe shoes swayed, and musical notes hung in delicate clusters from pink and green silken ribbons. Ornamental bulbs of green and pink were traced in silver, and tiny white lights illuminated the entire affair.

Stevie and Nae Nae took turns leading Kylie and Ian to each tree. They ate cotton candy and the two little ones rode on Santa's railroad twice. Afterward, they rode the people mover around to Greektown and went to Nikki's Pizzeria. All the while Kylie peered at Ian now and again trying to still the anxiety in her stomach and the racing of her heart, which was happening far too often for a trip to the Festival of Lights. She kept thinking, *Are we going to have sex tonight? Do I want to go through with this?* She could only focus on what was going on in front of her for a few minutes at a time, then she was off worrying again.

When they got home, Jillian was there, and she took over the children and reminded Kylie to be home by midnight. Before Kylie knew it, they were back at Ian's.

"Come on," Ian said as he took her hand and led her to his bedroom. Once inside he flicked on his CD player, which emitted slow rhythmic music into the air. He went back and shut the door behind them. "Let me take that for you," he said as he reached for her coat and tossed it aside. "You wanna dance?" he asked her.

Kylie just nodded and he took her into his arms and pressed her tightly against him. The music went through them, and they moved each other slowly around the small space between the bed and the chair. Ian bent his head to kiss her and thought for a moment of that other boy Terrance, who wanted to be near Kylie like this. She slowed the kiss down, and he liked the change. He forgot himself as they swayed. He felt the small delicate bones of her back beneath his hands, the soft flesh, the slight contour of her waist, and the feel of her buttocks in his hands. He kept his hands there and pressed her against him. He didn't even want to hurry it anymore, this was nice. The next part would come, he could feel it, and he could wait the little bit of time until then.

When he pulled his mouth away he heard her breathing

and his, it was soft and quick, like cats panting. She took the next kiss and her lips were already warm, moist, and soft after their first long kiss. What he loved about her kisses was that there seemed to be something underneath the hot passion and the ready eagerness. She was telling him something. Something true, and sweet, and deep. And he felt that he was close to making out the meaning inside her kisses. But not quite.

The minutes became liquid, suspended, and fluid, all at the same time. It had been some time since he had kissed for so long, where the kissing became the point. Many of his past sexual encounters had taken on the quality of business meetings. The kissing and petting were brief, like the businessman's handshake and greeting, all the quicker to get him what he wanted.

But it was different with Kylie. He felt like he could kiss Kylie all night. But they didn't have all night. His mother would be home around 1 A.M., her mother expected her home in a few hours, and he had to complete the challenge before the weekend was over.

"Ian, I like you so much," Kylie whispered to him.

His answer was a kiss.

After a bit they climbed onto the bed and Ian slipped his sweater off over his head. "Now you," he whispered. The lamp on his desk cast an intimate, dim light. She hesitated. "It's okay," he assured her. She paused longer, then, slowly pulled her sweater over her head. He placed a finger underneath each bra strap and slid them off her shoulders. "Don't look so scared."

"I can't help it."

"Here, I'll do it." He scooted in close and kissed her again, all the while deftly unfastening her bra. When he pulled back he slid the straps from her arms. "Is that so bad?"

"Yes."

"Oh, Kylie, it'll be okay, I promise." He started kissing her again and after a short while he wore only his underwear. She still wore her jeans, but they'd been unfastened and opened. Ian moved so that he sat on the side of the bed with his feet spread apart on the floor. "Come here," he said softly. Kylie slid off the bed and stood above him. He put his hands on her bare waist and looked up into her eyes in the dim light. She closed her eyes out of fear and embarrassment as he moved her jeans past her hips, then thighs, then she felt them fall around her ankles. "Help me out," he said, and she opened her eyes for a moment to find his shoulder. She placed her hand there, keeping her eyes off his, and pulled each foot out of her pants as he moved them away.

Her face felt hot all over as she lingered in this moment of standing nearly naked before a boy for the first time. Nothing clothed her except for a pair of pink cotton bikini panties. Her embarrassment was so huge that it nearly paralyzed her, and she had no idea what to do with herself. All that she could think was that she wanted some clothes on . . . badly.

"Girl, you look good!" Ian exclaimed softly. And because she heard the surprise in his voice she had to open her eyes and see the expression on his face. It was open and honest and she blushed furiously. Somehow his words and expression made her want to cover herself even more.

Ian stood then, and because she was already so close to him, their bodies were pressed together. She felt his arousal and felt self-conscious because of that, too. He kissed her lips twice and then they French-kissed for such a long time that Kylie almost forgot her fear because of the sweetness of his mouth. "I want to make love to you, Kylie," Ian said as he held her in his arms. And then all of it was back: her fear, embarrassment, and uncertainty. But underneath all of that was desire, too.

"All right," she whispered hesitantly, then shyly, "do you have something?"

"Yeah, I do, hold on." Kylie got back onto the bed and pulled the covers over herself. She felt safer that way. Ian removed a book from his bookshelf, opened it, and took out a condom that was wedged between the pages.

"That's quite a bookmark," Kylie joked. Ian just smiled and came back to the bed. He climbed under the covers with her and said her name softly before putting his hands in places that she had never let a boy touch before. His hands were gentle and insistent at the same time, and she felt his hand tugging hers off his shoulder and placing it on his brief-clad penis. She let him, and in the quiet darkness of his room, with the two of them alone in that house, she let her fears fall away for a moment as his hands coaxed hers. She couldn't say when, exactly, he moved her panties away, because he seemed to never stop kissing and caressing her, but she was entirely aware when he rose up and began taking off his underwear.

"Wait," she said.

"I just can't wait much longer, Kylie, I can't."

And she chose to believe him because to give in to the moment was far more pleasurable and easier than resisting it. She turned away when he started to put on the condom. What if he messes up, or can't get it on correctly, she worried. She didn't want to see that. Too embarrassing.

After he had the condom on, he reached over and turned the lamp off.

He lay atop her and began easing himself inside of her. When he pressed himself against her he felt how tight she was, and felt her tense up beneath him. "Are you okay?" he asked.

"Yes," she whispered. It hurt, but not nearly as much as she heard that it might. All during the time that he entered her she felt fear and anxiety, and very little pleasure.

He entered gently, slowly, keeping his weight off of her as much as possible. She began to move just as gently and slowly against him and after a while he felt himself fully inside of her. "Are you okay?" he asked again. He had never been so concerned about a girl's well-being when he was having sex with her. He had told himself before he picked her up that evening that he would not let himself think about the bet. Instead he would focus on the fact that he liked her and that she made him feel things, things he did not care to probe, that he had never felt before. Unlike nearly every other time that he'd had sex, with Kylie he felt suddenly and intensely tender. He didn't focus on the fact that his guilt may have been part of the reason that he wanted to please her so much.

"Are you still hurting?" he asked.

She listened to his breathing, warm against her ear, then said, "Not too much anymore."

He changed the rhythm of his strokes. "Do you like that?" His voice was barely above a whisper, his lips near her ear now.

She breathed a "Yes."

They went on like that, pressed together warm and intimate, kissing again and again. Kylie was surprised, she had expected to be frightened the entire time, but Ian was so tender that she had relaxed more than she had expected. When it was over he still lay atop her, and he felt the rhythm of her heartbeat thump, thump against the beat of his own, and it was as though he heard one heartbeat strung together, beating harder and faster. He kissed her mouth, then her cheek, then buried his lips into the hollow between her neck and shoulder. He didn't want to move, but he knew he must be getting heavy on her.

Ian pulled himself away carefully and lay on his back staring into the dark, feeling the heat of Kylie's body close to his. All he could think of was how, for the first time, his heart was in it while making love to a girl, and how it was all tainted by the challenge. Then he discarded the condom and told Kylie that he'd be right back. She heard water running just down the hall. He returned in a few minutes with a plush towel that he handed to her. "You know, in case you bled," he said softly.

"Thank you." She was not comfortable enough to do anything with it while Ian was lying there watching, though.

"Here, put it underneath you like this," he said. He

pulled the covers back and took the towel from her, and she rolled to one side while he laid the towel out, keeping it doubled. She had been lying in a wet spot, so she appreciated the dry comfort of the towel. "Do you want to wash up?"

Kylie nodded.

He went over to his closet and got out a long, thick, beige terry-cloth robe. "Here you go." After she put it on, he took her hand and led her to the bathroom. In the bathroom there was a linen closet, from it he took a blue washcloth and matching towel. "Just come to my room when you're done, okay?"

"Okay." When he'd gone and shut the door, Kylie pulled the robe off and looked at herself in the mirror. She searched for several long minutes, trying to see if she looked different from the way that she'd looked just a short while ago. She tried to see if her eyes looked worldlier, more mature now that she had had sex. She didn't look any different, but she felt different. Then she looked at the body that she hardly paid any attention to and tried to see it the way that Ian had when he had said she looked good. It was the same body, but she had never seen it as Ian had.

She shook her head with a small smile and got busy washing herself up. She had bled only a little, she'd thought there would be more. When she was done she wrapped herself in the robe, wrapped the washcloth in the towel, and carried them out with her.

When she came back to Ian's bedroom he was in bed, his covers pulled up to his waist, his chest bare. He pulled the covers back as an invitation to her, and she put the towel down in his desk chair and accepted.

"Aren't you going to take the robe off?" he said as he gently tugged at the lapel.

"No," she said with a giggle, clasping both sides of the lapel tightly and pulling it closely against her chest and neck.

"Come on, come on," he said with a smile as he gently pulled on the lapel again.

"No, now stop."

"All right." He gave her a kiss. "I thought that you would be different."

"Different how?"

"I don't know." He plucked at the robe as he spoke. "I thought that you'd be, you know, stiff or something."

"I wasn't?"

"No," he said looking her in the eyes. "Not at all. You felt good."

She blushed and so did he. "Yeah?" she asked.

"Yeah." He said the next words with his face nestled in her neck. "You felt so good, Kylie."

She did not know what to say to that. Nothing she thought of sounded right, and talking about it with him, right now, was not something that she was ready to do. So she said, "Ian, could you sing me some of the song you're going to sing at the winter talent contest?"

"Yeah?"

"Yeah."

"All right." Ian propped himself up on his elbow and began singing softly, but no less beautifully, the romantic ballad that he'd been practicing for the contest. He stopped singing after the first verse.

"More," Kylie urged softly. She lay on her back and her dark, dark eyes stared up into his, and she felt as if her heart were caught in her throat.

Ian sang the chorus. "'Hold on to the love, hold on to the dream, don't let it go away, do all you can to make it stay, baby. Hold on to the love, hold on to the dream, don't let it slip away, give all to make it stay, baby.'"

"That was *so* beautiful!" Kylie whispered.

"Thank you." He kissed her lips.

"Have you ever been in love, Ian?"

"No, I don't think so."

"You sang that like you've been in love before."

"I just sing it like I hear it."

"Like a parrot?" she teased.

"Yeah, like a parrot," he said, bopping her gently on the nose with his index finger. "Are you hungry?" he asked.

"No. What time is it?"

Ian leaned over and looked at the clock on his night-stand. "Ten-thirty."

"Ten-thirty," she echoed.

"You have to be back at twelve, right?"

"Mmmhmmm."

"What do you want to do now?"

She grinned at him. "Talk."

"Talk?"

"Yes, talk."

"All right." So they did, about home and school, and their friends. Once, while they were talking, he thought about the bet, and wondered how something that began for all the wrong reasons could end up making him feel so right. But then he pressed the thoughts from his mind and they messed around some more, but didn't have sex. Then it was nearly 11:30 P.M., so they got dressed and he drove Kylie home.

Once he dropped her off he wasn't in his car five minutes before he was already missing her.

Chapter 15

"Well?" Desiree demanded.

Kylie had asked Desiree if the three of them, Tracy, Dez, and Kylie could meet over her house. It was the day after Kylie had had sex with Ian and she needed to talk to her girls badly.

"Yeah, what is this all about?" Tracy wanted to know. Kylie had refused to tell them anything over the telephone. She just said that it was important and that she needed to talk to them face-to-face.

"I did it," Kylie said all in a breath.

"Did what?" Dez asked suspiciously. She was trying to decipher the dazed, dreamy look on Kylie's face.

"Ian and I, we did it."

"No! Shut the hell up! You didn't, Kylie," Tracy said, shocked.

"Oh Kylie, not with Ian Striver. Not him," Dez moaned.

"Don't say it like that. You don't know him. You don't know what he's like when we're alone."

"No, no I don't. But I do know that he ran around telling everyone about other girls that he slept with. I do know that his sorry behind had to drag himself over to talk to you in front of his friends when I was with you. I know all of that. And you do too, Kylie, so why are you trippin'?" Dez asked.

"Yeah, I know about all that. But if you could see him when he's alone with me, you'd understand. I think he's changed. I know that he cares about me. And I love being with him." Kylie sighed, her eyes still dreamy and happy.

Tracy looked at Dez and tried to give her a warning look that said, "Go easy."

"Kylie," Dez began, "we just don't want to see you get hurt. That's all, girl."

"I know."

"We want you to slow it down a little. You know, don't ignore all the stuff you've heard about him. Keep that in the back of your mind because you haven't known him that long."

"No, you haven't," Tracy said. "Two weeks, that's all."

"Three, actually," Kylie corrected.

"Three weeks ain't nothin', Kylie. It sure ain't enough time for you to know somebody before you give up your *virginity!*" Desiree admonished.

"Well, *I* thought so, okay," Kylie said with signs of anger.

"I thought so. I'm in this relationship, not you. I know what he says to me, how he says it, the way he holds and kisses me. Me! Or maybe that's the problem. You're so used to little ole Kylie being ignored by boys that you can't believe someone like Ian would want me."

"What did you say?" Now Desiree was angry. "I know that you didn't say that mess to me, Kylie. As long as we've been friends, that's how you see me? Huh?"

"Hold on now," Tracy urged.

"No, I ain't holdin' on nothing! Is that what you think of me?" Dez wanted to know.

"No," Kylie nearly whispered. "But you need to ease up. I don't need you attacking me right now, Dez. You don't always have to say the first damn thing that comes to your mind."

The girls sat together quietly for a couple of uncomfortable moments. Then Desiree said, "I'm sorry, Kylie."

"Me, too," Kylie said with tears in her eyes.

Desiree had tears in her eyes too. "You're my girl, that's all. I don't want that idiot screwin' with you . . . with your head, I mean." Then she giggled at her unintentional pun.

"I know," Kylie said as she reached out for a hug. "I love you too."

"Ya'll better not let this boy come between us!" Tracy said and she got up to join her two best friends in the hug.

Chapter 16

Mr. Striver's favorite restaurant specialized in seafood and steak and sat on a downtown corner not far from the crossing of Jefferson and Woodward. The decor of dark wood paneling, hardwood floors, broad mirrors, and small lamps held a classy masculine feel that was right up Mr. Striver's alley. The food was off the hook, too. They'd all ordered the same dinner of T-bone steak medium rare, shrimp scampi, and tossed Caesar salad. Old-school music played in muted tones with Earth, Wind and Fire were center stage right now. Their orders had arrived some time ago and they were nearly finished with their meals.

Ian could tell that his father had something to tell them. He could sense the uneasiness beneath his jokes, laughter, and anecdotes. He wished that his father would just get it over with already.

"So you're coming to Ian's talent show, huh?" Kim asked.

"Well, actually, I can't. I was going to tell you before we left, Ian," he said. Ian didn't say anything. He just looked at his father, his face expressionless. "It turns out that Kelsey does have a recital that same night. It's her first. Miranda thinks it's important that I be there. So do I."

Ian shrugged and looked away. He balled his napkin into a wad and let it drop into his plate. "That's cool. No big deal."

"I know that yours is important, too, Ian," Mr. Striver said.

"Hey, I said no biggie," Ian said.

"It's important," Kim said, her lips and voice tight, "just not *as* important, right, Daddy?"

"Of course it is, Kim. Don't turn this into something nasty," Mr. Striver said.

"Don't tell me what to do. Why don't you do the right thing if you don't want things to get nasty? How about that?"

"Kim, in life you have to make choices, and they're not all easy."

"That's right, Daddy. You have to make choices, and you've made yours, haven't you? Again. Kelsey has you all the time, every day. We see you *maybe* twice a month now that you're with Miranda. Twice a month! Ian invites you to his talent show and you can't make a sacrifice and come?"

128

Ian wanted to cheer his sister on. She was saying what they both had felt for years. But he somehow felt numb and separated from what was happening.

"Let's go," Ian said.

Ian and Kim got into their coats and waited near the door of the restaurant while their father paid the bill. Ian was almost comforted by the bite in the air when they walked out and headed for his father's Ford Explorer. The ride home was mercifully brief, and nothing but the sound of the radio broke the silence until they were parked in front of the house that they had all lived in together for nearly twelve years, before Mr. Striver had left to make a new life for himself.

"Here," he said to Kim, who sat beside him in the front. Ian saw him put money into her hand. Kim took the money in silence, opened the door, and allowed a mumbled thanks before she shut the door behind herself. "Wait," Mr. Striver said as Ian opened the back door.

"I'm sorry, Ian." He held money out for Ian, too.

"Yeah. See you later."

His mother was probably still out with her friends, because she wasn't home when they got inside. It was just as well; her temper was sometimes as volatile as Kim's when it came to their father. Ian didn't feel like retelling it all right now anyway. Kim was already in her room, and he headed straight to his. He tossed the money on his dresser, and it wasn't until the next day that he unfolded the money that his father had given him. It was two fifty-dollar bills.

A one-hundred-dollar payoff.

"Now explain this to me again," Kylie said. Monday afternoon, a white sky that characterized southeastern Michigan winter found Ian and Kylie less than five minutes from her place. Ian had met her at her locker after classes, and they'd headed out in his car.

"I told you, Kim wanted you to come over."

"Your sister wants me to come over? Why again?"

"I don't know. Just to hang out. No big deal." Ian didn't tell Kylie that after they made love, he had ended up talking to Kim about her. He didn't tell Kim the truth about everything. He didn't tell Kim about the bet or the sex or how much he liked Kylie. But Kim knew him well enough to know that if he bothered to talk about a girl for the length of a whole conversation, then something significant was going on.

When they got to Ian's house Kim was singing along with hip-hop diva Diana Love. They came into the kitchen and Kylie had to smile because Kim was jammin', doing some of Diana's best moves, and doing them well. Kim smiled and waved at them, never missing a beat. Ian jumped right in with his sister and started dancing with her. Years of sister/brother duos showed in every step.

"What's up?" Kim said to Kylie after the song was over.

"What's up?" Kylie greeted her in return.

"I like me some Diana Love," Kim said. "So have a seat, Kylie." Kylie sat down at the table where Kim had some hairstyle magazines laid out.

"Do you like doing hair?" Kylie asked.

"Yeah, most of the time. I make good money, and I like seeing the end results after I've taken care of someone. It gets to be hard on my back toward the end of a long day. I'm good at it though, I get a lot of referrals from my clients."

"That's cool."

"So you like this blockhead?" Kim asked as she shoved Ian playfully.

"Yeah, I guess so," Kylie said with a smile.

"He's okay," Kim said. "He's got his good points."

"I have a lot of good points, woman!" Ian said.

"Now don't get carried away," Kim teased. "So, you want me to tell you some stuff about Ian from when he was little?" she asked with a mischievous look in her eyes.

"Ooooh, yes! Tell me."

Kim laughed lightly. "All right, let me tell you about the Easter hunt that he went on when he was four years old."

"Don't tell her that stupid story, Kim!"

Kim took a moment to swat Ian with a comb. "I will so! So Ian's four, right, and we're visiting our aunt's church for Easter. After church they had this huge Easter egg hunt planned. The weather was nice and they headed all of us outside. Well, Ian was this bad little boy anyway . . ."

"Wait now, I was not bad! Active. Maybe busy. But not bad!" Ian said.

"Whatever. He used to get into everything. So anyway, Ian wanders off trying to find eggs in 'special' places and ends up wandering his little behind back into the church, where he proceeds to fall asleep under a pew. Well, everyone's looking for him, my mama and auntie are scared to death, and I'm hollerin', 'where's my baby brother, where's my baby brother?' and cryin' my eyes out. Grown-ups have started walking up and down the street yellin', 'Ian! Ian!' And just when some-body's about to call the police somebody thinks to go inside and start lookin'. Well, my mother is, like, 'Call the police anyway, and still keep lookin'.' So that's what we do. People head into the church callin' Ian and he hears them and wakes up. There he is curled up under the pew lookin' all cute in his Easter suit with his eyes all sleepy. Everybody's grabbin' on him and laughing, my mama was cryin' and laughin' at the same time. The pastor said, most folks are out trying to find eggs today, his church was blessed to find a child."

Kylie laughed at the story and at Ian's embarrassment at the adorable depiction of him.

"I hate that story," Ian grumbled with a small smile. Ian pulled out some chips, sodas, and playing cards and the three sat around talking and laughing and playing tunk.

After a while Kim said, "Ian, did you take out all the trash like Mama told you to?"

"Damn, I forgot."

"You've got a dirty mouth, boy. You better go ahead and get that out of the way."

As soon as Ian left the room Kim turned to Kylie and asked, "Who does your hair?"

Kylie wasn't expecting the question. "Umm, this lady named Gwen, when I get to go."

"How often do you get to go?"

"I don't know, maybe every few months."

Kim shook her head. "You have to go more often than that if you've got a perm."

"I know, but I can't."

"Money?"

"Yeah."

"I could fix you up, if you want. Your ends are all broken off and your hair is extra dry from all that gel you put on it. I could give you a good touch-up, shampoo, deep conditioning. You've got real nice hair."

Kylie made a face. To her, it was too thick and too nappy.

"No, you do. It's thick, and you've got a lot of it. If it were healthy it would look great. I could give you a real good cut, too. Something that accentuated those eyes of yours."

"That would be great, but . . ."

"I'd do it for free the first time."

"No, I couldn't. If I can't pay you, I'd just rather not."

"Don't be stupid. I like you. I like doing hair, and I'd love to see what I could do with yours. I could do it for you every few weeks too, and you could help me out in the shop a few hours on Saturdays to pay for it."

"For real?" Kylie asked, becoming a little hopeful.

"For real. Ian hardly ever brings any girls home. The few that I have met were way too stuck-up. You're nice. I always wished that I had a little sister, somebody's hair to do, somebody to teach some things to, you know."

"Yeah."

"So anyway, we'll just start by having me do your hair. We'll see how it goes from there. How does that sound?"

"Cool. Real cool."

"Okay, have Ian bring you over after school tomorrow. I'll hook you up then."

Ian came back just then. "What took you so long?" Kim asked.

"None of a your business, bossy." Ian winked at Kylie. She told him that it was time for her to go and he took her home.

Kylie talked to her mother about Kim's proposal and Jillian said that it would be fine. Kylie was excited. She couldn't stand her hair, had always fantasized about making it better, and now here was a chance. Kylie had never seen anyone's hair that Kim had done, but nearly anything would be better than what she had.

The next day Ian drove Kylie to his house to get her hair done. He told her that he would be hanging out with some of his friends while she was busy and return in a couple of hours to take her home. They sat outside in the driveway for a few minutes kissing, then he let her inside the house, saw her to the kitchen where Kim was waiting for her, and left.

Kim and Kylie had a good time together. They kept the radio on while they talked and Kim worked expertly on Kylie's hair. Kim told Kylie a couple more stories about Ian, and then some about herself. The room became fragrant with the shampoo and conditioners that Kim used. For Kylie, the two hours passed easily, and with no mirror in the room the progress of her hair remained a pleasant mystery. Kim showed Kylie some really nice cuts that she felt would be cute on her; Kylie picked one and watched as small clippings of her hair fell to her lap and the floor. Then there was the hot smell of her hair being curled, and all too soon Kim was saying, "All done."

Kylie felt butterflies in the pit of stomach. She had come to expect a lot from this time with Kim and from Kim's efforts on her hair. "The bathroom is down the hall on the right. Go ahead and look," Kim said with a smile.

Kylie got up, but before she could make it out of the kitchen she heard someone coming in the door. Ian rounded the corner into the kitchen and stopped, his eyes widening. The expression on his face made Kylie blush, and even before she had seen herself, she felt wonderful, because Ian's face told her that she looked good.

"Damn," Ian said under his breath.

"I know," Kim said. "She looks good, doesn't she?"

"Yeah."

"I haven't even seen it myself," Kylie said a bit shyly.

"Go 'head," Kim urged.

Kylie eased past Ian and made her way to the bathroom. She flicked on the light and went to stand before the mirror. Before she could stop herself Kylie broke into a wide grin. She had never looked so good. Her hair was shiny and black, three inches shorter, and shorn of all the ragged broken ends. It looked thick and healthy. Kim had cut and blow-dried it into a sleek look that grazed her shoulders, framed her face nicely, and accentuated her eyes just as Kim had promised. The perm that Kim had used on her hair gave her an excellent touch-up. Kylie swung her head tentatively and her hair swung a beat behind. She did it again and then again. She ran her fingers through her hair and felt its lightness and softness. "Wow," she whispered.

She went back to the kitchen where Ian and Kim were, and before she even thought she went across the kitchen and gave Kim a hug. "Thank you so much. I love it."

Kim laughed, "You're welcome, girl. I told you, you have really great hair. Thick and heavy. We just have to keep it healthy."

"So do you want me to come this Saturday?" Kylie asked.

"Yeah, that sounds good. I can pick you up at eight-thirty and you can work until noon. How does that sound?"

"Sounds good to me. Well, I better go. Thanks again, Kim."

"That's all right. Now wrap it every night when you're going to bed."

"Okay," Kylie said.

Kylie and Ian headed out and Kim stayed behind in the kitchen. Ian got her coat out of the closet and helped her into it. They stood facing one another in the semidarkness of the small foyer, close together.

"You look really good," Ian said softly.

"Thanks."

"And your eyes, they're like midnight."

"Thanks," Kylie whispered back.

He lowered his head and she raised hers, and their lips met for the kiss that each of them had wanted from the moment that he walked into the kitchen. He raised his hands and cupped her face in his hands as he felt the warmth of the kiss course through his body. Kylie wrapped her arms inside his open coat and then Ian tilted her backward and she felt the wall behind her. He stepped between her legs and pressed himself against her and she felt herself melting into him.

"Y'all gone?" Kim called from the kitchen.

Ian gave Kylie two quick kisses before he answered, "Almost." Kim put on another CD and Ian kissed Kylie one more slow, deep time before he opened the door to the outside without a word and let them both out. Kylie felt the cool air move over her newly straightened hair and felt it sway gently in the breeze. She subconsciously smoothed it down with her hand and took in the fading sunlight and the deepening sky. Ian unlocked her door and held it for her while she got in. She remembered that when they first went out he hadn't opened the door for her.

"Your sister is really cool to do this for me," Kylie said after they had been driving for a bit, listening to music.

"Yeah, Kim is cool, period," Ian said as he glanced over at Kylie.

"She is. Did she tell you that I would be helping her at the shop and in exchange she would keep doing my hair for me?"

"Yeah, she did. That's tight." Ian had not thought through what would happen between Kylie and Kim. He hadn't thought a lot of things through.

Ian had reported on the results of his challenge to the FBI guys while Kylie got her hair done. He told his boys that he had accomplished both parts of his challenge, and that he would have tangible proof by the next day. He hadn't felt proud of himself, even worse, he'd felt guilty. He recalled the casual looks of amusement on the other guys' faces and felt sick again at the realization that he had put those expressions there by betraying this girl who had touched his heart and who constantly occupied his thoughts.

He tried to match up the soft feel of her against him and the easy trust that she had given him to the way that he was manipulating her, and he knew that it didn't fit. It wasn't supposed to fit.

He did not deny to himself that he liked Kylie a lot, he knew that he did. But he had reasoned with his guilty conscience that he was sixteen, not twenty-six, and much too young to worry about making a commitment to any girl. His main objective was to have fun, and as much of it as he possibly could. And that's all that he and Kylie were doing, having some fun. So, he wondered, if he was having so much fun, why wasn't he happy?

"Hello, there," Kylie joked. "You're getting pretty quiet."

Ian turned and saw her smile, and with only a little effort, he managed to give her one back. "Just thinking about stuff."

"Like what?"

"Nothing important."

"Oh." They were both quiet for a couple of minutes. "Do you want to do something this weekend?" Kylie asked.

"Um, I don't know. Let's hold up and I'll let you know. My mother was talking like she had something planned. Probably just more work for me," he tried to joke. She smiled innocently and Ian felt a sharp stab of guilt. Of course he planned to already have made this relationship history by the weekend. He just hoped that a girl as quiet as Kylie would let it die quietly when the time came.

Chapter 17

That night Ian wrote Kylie a letter that was more honest than he intended.

> Dear Kylie,
> I've been thinking about you a lot. More than I should probably, considering I need to get my grades up. I'm not going to lie to you, I never expected to care about you so much so quickly. But I do. I really do. When we made love the other night it felt so right, but don't misunderstand. That's not the only reason that you mean so much to me. I like talking to you, making you laugh, and

spending time with you. Even before you let me inside of you I had feelings for you.

Things are about to get really crazy for me in a minute. I've got the talent show coming up, so me and my boys will be practicing a lot, and I got to do some real studying before school gets seriously out of hand. So I won't be seeing you as much. But that won't stop me from thinking about you. Write me back.

Peace,

Ian

Ian had stopped by her locker the next morning and handed her this folded piece of loose-leaf paper. He hadn't stayed but a moment, and she had hurried off to first hour. She didn't read it first hour because they were doing a lab in science and she had to concentrate and participate. She didn't read it second hour because her English teacher didn't play. If she found you doing something other than her work she would take the offending object from you—whether it was homework for another class or whatever—hold it until the end of the day, and make you stay for a while after school for a lengthy lecture. So, it wasn't until third-hour history that she was able to read the letter. Once she did read it she had to read it again. She couldn't believe it. She wanted to shout out loud, or sing her favorite song, or hurry to Dez and Tracy and say, "See, this is how he feels about me." She wanted to do all of it, plus see him right away and tell him that she felt exactly the same.

She read the letter one more time, slowly. Mr. Rivers, her civics teacher, hardly paid attention once he gave the assignment. So she didn't have to worry about him bugging her while she got her romantic groove on. He wants me to write back, she thought. Okay, what to say and how to say it, she wondered?

> *Dear Ian,*
>
> *When I read your note I was so touched. I care about you a whole lot, too. I know that we've only been talking for a little while, but I think about you all the time. Sometimes I have to catch myself because I've drifted off thinking about you. I have never felt about any guy the way that I feel about you. It means so much to me that you feel the same way.*
>
> *Of course you know that what we did Friday night was a first for me. I am not sorry that you were my first. I never knew anything could feel that way. When we kissed that first time a few weeks ago under the winter sky, I thought it was beautiful. What we shared just a couple of days ago is almost unreal.*
>
> *I know that you said you're going to be busy for a while. But I hope that does not mean too busy for me. We could always study together, I know that I need to work harder in school. I'm writing you this letter when I should be doing my civics assignment! ☺*
>
> *I cannot wait to see you . . . and hold you . . . and*

kiss you. I've never written a letter like this before. I
never had a reason to.

    Love,
    Kylie

During lunch Kylie told Dez and Tracy that they had to get a table to themselves because she had something important to talk to them about. They tried to be alone at another table but some of their regular lunch buddies just plopped down, accepting the new lunching area with barely a bat of an eyelash. When the three girls went into the lunch line Kylie handed her friends the letter from Ian. She didn't tell them not to tell anyone, that went without saying, and they would never betray one another's confidence, ever.

"Damn, girl," Tracy and Dez said at the same time.

"What?" asked Melissa, a lunch table friend who had just gotten in line behind them.

"Nothing," Tracy said as she slipped Kylie the letter behind her back.

"What do you mean, 'nothing'? That doesn't make sense," Melissa persisted.

"Dang, girl!" Dez said with one of her pretty smiles. "You're so nosy. We were talking about Juan, he just walked by looking even finer than usual."

Melissa spotted Juan crossing the huge cafeteria and said, "Yeah, you're right, damn!" All four girls giggled and Tracy and Dez gave Kylie a secret sign that they would write her. After picking up their orders they joined the other kids at their table and talked and joked the hour away. Kylie's mind was only partially on the conversations that moved around her, no one seemed to notice much. But she was so distracted that the bell at the end of the hour surprised her. Tracy and Desiree wrote during the next hour, and Kylie read the letters behind her textbook.

Kylie,

Girl, I know that you're happy to get that note from Ian, and it does sound good, I'll give you that. It sounds real good, to tell the truth. But I still want you to watch your back. Ian was a wanna-be player before this, and he might be one now. I still don't like the way he dissed you in front of his friends. That was just flat-out wrong and ugly. But, even with all that, I hope that his note is truth, I hope that he has really changed. Because I could not stand it if he hurt you. I can see how those pretty eyes might make you forget good sense when you two are all up close and personal. ☺ Seriously, if you're happy, I want to be happy for you, if he hurts you, I'll hate him with you! You and Tracy are my girls, 4ever and 4always, 4real. Did you write him back?

Peace and hair grease, Dez

Dear Kylie,

Dez already told me what she's going to say. Doom and gloom, doom and gloom. Don't worry about it, girl. She loves you, you know that. But Dez is pretty as hell and always getting hit on by some boy, so she's sort of jaded. And yeah, there were those messed-up things that we heard about Ian from last year. But it may not all be true. That's the thing about rumors, maybe they're true, maybe they're not. Have you asked him about it?

Anyway, my main point is this: trust your instincts, girl. If your feelings for him are strong and true, enjoy it. And if you feel in your gut that his feelings for you are strong and true, enjoy them. I wish that you all had not used the V-ticket already. But it's done now. Your virginity is so precious, I hope that you gave it a lot of thought before you did the deed.

What was it like, anyway?

You know I'm for you, all the time and in the meantime. Tracy

That was the thing, Kylie admitted to herself, she wasn't exactly sure what her instincts were telling her. She couldn't tell if the voice inside of her that sang "I love Ian, I love Ian," was the voice of her instincts or whether the one that asked "Why doesn't he talk to you around his friends or ask you to hang out with his friends?" was the real voice. Or could both be true?

Chapter 18

Fifth-hour lunch period found Ian and five other members of
FBI seated side by side at a table with Tricia and her girlfriends. They bantered loudly as they consumed pale fries,
spicy chicken wings, and brightly colored sodas. Soon
though, the FBI members gathered at the end of one table for
a semiprivate powwow. "So what's the final report?" Dante
asked Ian.

"It's all good," he said. "Here it is, my ticket to the Freak
Fest," Ian said, flashing a smile and suppressing his feelings of
guilt. He wanted to get this part over with as quickly as possible. He pulled Kylie's letter out of his back jeans pocket and
handed it to Dante. Dante began reading it aloud to the other
guys. "Hey, not so loud!" Ian interrupted.

"What the hell do you care?" Dante asked.

"It ain't all that, man. It's just that we don't want everybody knowing our FBI business, do we?" Ian lied. Dante read the letter in lowered tones then. When he finished reading, the boys began hooting and laughing and giving Ian plays.

"Oh, you the man," Zaire said.

"Yeah, I got to hand it to you, Ian," Christian said, "only three weeks and you worked a whammy on this girl from the sounds of this letter."

Dante passed Ian back the letter. "Yeah, brother, you're all right. You handled your business. You're in good now, Ian."

Ian wasn't sure if his reflexes were slowed because he was distracted by his boys' compliments, Dante's assurance that he was in good with FBI, or the brush of Tricia's breasts against the back of his neck as she eased up behind him. But before he knew it the letter was out of his hands and in hers.

"What you got here, Ian?" Tricia asked.

"Nothing. Give that back, girl."

"Give what back? I thought you said that it was nothing?" she teased with a smile that would have captivated Ian some other time. But all he could think of was that enough people had seen Kylie's letter. He didn't want it to receive any more exposure.

"Give it back, Tricia."

"Just a minute. I want to see what's got you boys so interested over here. Maybe I'd be interested, too." As she spoke she backed away from the table and Ian got up to follow her. As he advanced toward her, Tricia began reading the letter aloud. "'Dear Ian, when I read your note I was so touched.'"

Her voice took on a drippy, singsong quality that made Ian cringe. All the kids at their two tables were listening, and a couple kids from a nearby table were drawn in by all of the commotion. He lunged for the note, but Tricia pivoted and turned her back toward him, stuck her behind out, stretched her torso, and extended the note further from Ian by holding it an arm's length away. She continued reading in a louder voice and Ian could just make out her words, Kylie's sweet words, over the blood thumping inside his ears.

Tricia, realizing that her time with the letter would be limited, jumped to the next paragraph. "'What we did Friday night was a first for me, I am not sorry that you were my first. I never knew that anything could feel that way.'"

"Stop it, Tricia, damn. Give it here!" Now Ian had her by the waist with one arm and he had grabbed the hand holding the letter with his other hand.

"Who *is* this?" Tricia wondered aloud. She looked at the end of the letter and read aloud, "'Love, Kylie.' Love Kylie?" she asked with a perplexed look at Ian.

"Look out, Ian," Dante said behind him. Ian glanced up to see Mr. Handle, one of the fifth-hour lunchroom monitors, heading their way, a stern expression screwed onto his face. Ian snatched the letter from Tricia and released her.

"Oooh, Ian," Tricia cooed. "You nasty boy!"

Ian just shook his head and tried to laugh with everybody else.

"Is that the girl that's been sniffing around our lockers, Ian?" Tricia asked. "The sweet, little pathetic puppy that you wouldn't even throw a bone to?" Then she giggled. "Oops,

147

sorry, I guess you did give her a bone, huh, lover boy?"

"Got that right," Zaire said giving Christian and Dante plays.

Ian felt sick. For a split second he thought about the damage that Kylie could do to him if she allowed his letter to be seen by others. But he didn't have the stomach or the time to worry about that. "You didn't really have sex with that girl, did you, Ian?" Tricia asked.

"You just read it, didn't you? He did the deed," Tricia's friend Kelli said.

Tricia looked slightly hurt. "Is that true?"

Ian just looked at her, then away.

"Damn," she nearly whispered. "Damn, Ian. Let's go, y'all," she said to her girls. All the ladies started gathering their things and in a few uncomfortable moments they were relocating themselves across the large cafeteria.

"Don't worry about it, Ian," Dante said. "She had no business snatching your stuff and reading it. It was never any of her business. Maybe she's learned a lesson."

"Yeah," Ian said distracted. Perfect, he thought, positively perfect. Now, not only had he given Kylie's letter to his boys, it had been read aloud before more people who were sure to spread the news. And now, Tricia was acting all hurt because he had had sex with Kylie. Damn! Ten minutes ago, his world was in balance and now everything was spinning totally out of control.

"I'll be back," Ian said to no one in particular at his table. He went over to where Tricia was now sitting. "Can I talk to you, Tricia?"

"Talk," she said sulkily.

"Privately, please."

She scooted out of the booth that she was in and followed him over to a window that looked out on a sunny winter day. They stood face-to-face. "Why are you mad at me, Tricia?" he asked in a soft, husky voice. He kept his eyes locked on to hers. He did like her, not like he liked Kylie, not even close, but he liked her.

"You know why."

"Tell me, so that I don't get it wrong."

"Because you're going around screwing little skank skeezers!" Her eyes were both angry and hurt, and her voice was slightly raised.

"But why does that make you mad? We're not even talking. You won't even give me *that* much play." He kept his voice low and seductively intimate; when she spoke again her voice matched his. He felt the thought, unwanted and unbidden, but clear as the tone of bell: everything had flipped because Tricia was now the girl with whom he was playing a role.

"We *could* be talking."

"Tell me that we *are* talking and you won't have to worry about me sexin' anybody else." She was so pretty, he thought, missing the time when that had been enough.

She smiled at his offer. "Promise?"

"Promise. Cross my heart," he said crossing his heart, "and cross yours, too," he said forming a cross just barely above Tricia's left breast. She liked it despite herself. She grabbed his finger in midair and held it gently in her hand.

"You better mean it, Ian Striver, 'cause I really do like you, boy." Then she gave him the smile that he wanted to see. He let out a small sigh of relief. He hoped that she didn't notice.

"I mean it," or at least I want to mean it, he thought. Then he pulled her hand toward him by the finger that she held and kissed it with a lingering, warm kiss. "I do."

"Why'd you have sex with *her* anyway?" Tricia asked. Tricia's emphasis on *her* confirmed all Ian's worse judgments about why he could never be serious with a girl like Kylie.

"You won't tell anyone?"

"No."

"Somebody dared me to do it."

"That's the only reason?"

"Why else would I do it?" And for an instant, Ian felt the taste of guilt, like bile at the back of his throat.

When Ian got back to his table his boys stopped their banter to check him out. "How did it go?" Dante asked.

"It went all right. We're officially talking now," Ian said, unable to force a smile.

"Damn, man, how'd you do that?" Christian asked.

"When you left here five minutes ago you were in the doghouse because she found out in front of God and everyone that you had slept with another girl. Now y'all talkin'? I guess by the end of the day she'll be your lady, huh?" All of the fellas started laughing.

"Shut up," Ian said. "I don't want her thinking that we're laughing at her."

"We are laughing at her. She should have more sense than to trust your ass," Zaire said with a laugh. Ian laughed right along with them, but he felt nauseous. Is this who he wanted to be, he asked himself, someone that even his boys knew couldn't be trusted by a girl?

No. Definitely not.

"Ian, hold on a second," Mr. Hill said.

Ian was on his way to history after lunch when Mr. Hill spotted him on the fifth floor. "Hey, Mr. Hill, what are you doing up here?"

"Looking for you, actually. Your mother called and requested a progress report on you, so I thought I'd come up and give it to you."

"Oh, thanks. I forgot to come and get it."

"Are you sure you forgot?"

"For real. My grades are looking all right, I want her to see that I'm improving."

"That's good to hear." He looked at Ian for a few seconds as kids hurried past to class. The tardy bell would ring in less than a minute. "What's the matter then?"

"Nothing." It was like Mr. Hill had radar, Ian thought.

"What's the matter?"

"Nothing, really. I just have a lot on my mind right now. I got some stuff I'm trying to sort out, that's all. Nothing to do with school."

"Sometimes stress with things that don't have to do with school can impact how a person does in their classes."

"Who mentioned stress? All I said was that I have some things I'm sorting out." The tardy bell sounded, soon it was quiet around them with only a few stragglers making their way through the hall. Both of them ignored the people moving past them.

"I'll just say this then, and let you go for now: if you handle problems early on or get help with them early on, they don't have to become overwhelming."

"I'm late, Mr. Hill."

"I'll see you to your class." They walked two doors down to Ian's class. Mr. Hill said hello to the history teacher and told him that Ian had been with him, and the history teacher said that that was fine. "Just a moment," Mr. Hill said as Ian stood at the threshold of the door. Ian turned back and took a step into the hallway.

"Stop by my office before you leave today."

"If I have time. See ya, Mr. Hill."

"No problem, Ian. Later."

"That's messed up, what Ian Striver did to your girl," Courtney Nelson said as she took her seat next to Tracy in their seventh-hour Algebra III class.

"What are you talking about?" Tracy asked as she tried to fish a pencil from the bottom of her bag.

"He read her letter out loud in the cafeteria. Or rather, he let Tricia Connors read it out loud." Courtney shook her head solemnly at the vagaries of adolescent boys. "Now it's like everybody knows that she and Ian had sex, and Tricia's telling everybody that Ian had to do it as a dare, and that's the only reason Ian's been talking to Kylie."

"What?" Tracy asked in a tight, disbelieving whisper. This was a nightmare. This was worse than even Desiree had imagined things getting. "Who told you all this?"

"I was right there, sitting next to their table in the cafeteria. I heard her read the letter myself. Then I heard all the stuff Tricia said about the dare in the hallway on my way to class," Courtney said. "Like I said, that's messed up."

"Damn, tell me about it!" Tracy said just as the teacher began the lesson. This was going to knock Kylie on her butt. Ian must be a certified monster to do something like this, Tracy thought.

As soon as Tracy got out of math she made a beeline for the lockers where she knew Kylie would be getting ready to go home. As Tracy neared their lockers she half hoped that Kylie wouldn't be there, and she wouldn't have to tell her friend the bad news. But Kylie was there, alone, arranging her books in her bag.

"What's up, Tracy?" Kylie said pleasantly when her friend stopped beside her.

"We need to talk, Kylie."

Kylie stopped moving at the note of urgency in her friend's voice. "What's the matter?" Kylie said, trying to fight the small tight feeling of dread that was forming in the pit of her stomach.

"Ian is one of the lowest things to walk the planet, girl."

"Tracy, what happened?"

"Girl, Courtney Nelson, you know her, right?"

"Yeah."

"She says Ian passed your letter around at lunch today, then he let that girl Tricia Connors, the one we see him with sometimes, read it, and now Tricia is going around saying that Ian just slept with you on a dare."

"What? It's got to be a rumor, right? Or Courtney got it wrong or something? It can't be true, can it, Tracy?" Kylie wanted to cry. Even if Courtney got some of it wrong, or it was just a rumor, some part of it *had* to be right in order for Courtney to have that much information. And *any* part of it that was true was simply too damn much, Kylie thought. She shook her head from side to side, her eyes closed, tears pressing close beneath her lids. God, God, God. Why had she trusted him? Why had he done this to her? "Oh, Tracy, I loved him," Kylie whispered. And Tracy wanted to slap Ian across the face because of the anguish she heard in her friend's voice. "I still do."

"Don't you cry, Kylie, not over him. Please, girl."

"What's up?" Desiree said as she approached from behind Kylie. She was escorted by Chris Kimpson, fine and smart, and pathetically boring. Desiree took in the look on Tracy's face and Kylie's stiff back, and told Chris, "I'll talk to you later, okay?"

"Okay. Can I get your number, though?"

"Let's talk later," she said dismissing him impatiently. When he'd walked away she said again, "What's up?" This time it wasn't a greeting but a query.

Kylie turned around then, and when Desiree saw Kylie's face her own face hardened. "Tell me this isn't about Ian Striver."

"It is, and I can't take an 'I told you so' right now, Dez," Kylie said, her voice trembling.

"I'm not going to do that to you, girl," Dez said.

"Because, of course, you did tell me so. Oh, you were *sooo* right about Ian!" Kylie said.

"Well, I'm not happy to be right," Dez said as she stroked her friend's back. "I was hoping all along that I would be wrong, Kylie, believe me."

"I do."

"What happened?" Desiree asked. Kylie and Tracy told Dez everything that they'd heard. "That piece of trash!" Desiree said when the girls were done.

"So what now?" Tracy asked.

"She has to get in his face," Dez said furiously.

"Damn. No. I don't want to," Kylie said.

Tracy said, "You have to, Kylie. You need to find out what he said, if his lying behind will tell the truth."

"Probably not," Kylie and Dez interrupted in unison.

"Then you have to get some things off of your chest. If you don't, it will just eat at you, because there will be all of these things that you *wish* you could have said," Tracy continued.

"She's right," Dez said.

"Of course, we'll be there for you, you won't have to face his backstabbing, two-faced behind by yourself, that's for damn sure," Tracy said.

"You got *that* right!" Dez concurred.

"Thanks, y'all." Kylie bit her lower lip for a moment, considering. "Okay, let's do this and get it over with," Kylie said as she took a deep breath.

"Right now?" Dez asked.

"Might as well. No real reason to wait, is there?" Kylie asked.

"No, I guess not," Dez said.

"Let's go see if we can find him, then," Tracy said.

Kylie's heart beat hard and fast as she walked between her friends. While she wanted to get it over with, she most certainly was not looking forward to confronting Ian. She had no idea how he might react. The things that Tracy had told her about Ian were still buzzing around in her head like dangerous wasps. Each word stung. He let another girl read her letter. He allowed her to read it in front of people in the *cafeteria*, for God's sake! He let all those people know that she had lost her virginity with him? How could he do that? Did he do that? Did he tell this girl that he only had sex with her on a dare. A dare . . . please, please, please don't let that be true, she prayed. Why was Tricia getting so much information about them? Was she just a good friend, or were he and Tricia talking? She sifted through her mind the times that she had seen Ian and Tricia together. But she couldn't remember how intimate the two had seemed.

Much too soon they were approaching Ian where he stood with all of his friends in front of their lockers. The group was in no particular hurry to leave at the end of their school day. There was Ian with his friends, and there was Tricia near him, talking to a group of girls. He was turned away from the stairs and did not seem to see her coming. Kylie's stomach tightened involuntarily and her palms felt clammy and cold. She licked her dry lips and wiped her palms discreetly on her blue jeans.

"Wait for me here," she told her friends when they'd cleared the stairs.

"All right," Dez said, and she and Tracy took up position across the hall from Ian and his group.

"Ian, it's your girlfriend," a boy Kylie thought was named Michael said in a nasty tone of voice. She flicked him a quick glance before focusing her attention back on Ian. Ian turned toward her then and his expression changed from the easier, relaxed one he held as he conversed with his friends, to an unreadable mask.

"Can I talk to you alone?" Kylie said when she approached him. Tricia moved over to stand beside him. Get the hell away, Kylie thought.

"I'm about to go. I'll have to talk to you later," Ian said, keeping his tone and face calm and closed off.

"I need to talk to you *now*."

Ian hesitated a moment and then said, "All right, come on." He walked her down the hall just beyond earshot of their friends. "What's up?" he asked, clearly not wanting to know.

"What's all this that I'm hearing, Ian?" Kylie was unable to keep a small quiver out of her voice. Why was he behaving so coldly? Why did he look at her as though she were a stranger wasting his valuable time?

"I don't know, what are you hearing?"

It took her a moment to open her mouth, to let the words escape and live between them.

"That you passed my letter around. That you let Tricia read it out loud in the cafeteria."

"And?" Ian felt cold all over, but he found that if he just didn't meet her eyes the cold didn't hurt so much. Why couldn't she just hate him and go away? he thought. That would end this for her and for him; he had never wanted anything so much in his life as he wanted this conversation to end.

Kylie swallowed. Who the hell was this boy? "Is it true?"

Ian looked above her head at the display case across the hall from them for a moment, then back at Kylie. "Yeah."

Kylie nodded her head slowly as she looked at Ian's shoulder, her hands, then down the hallway where her friends watched her anxiously, and finally into Ian's eyes. "Why?"

"Look, Kylie, we were just kickin' it, okay? Don't blow it all out of proportion. It was nice, now it's over. No big deal."

"No big deal." She looked into his eyes trying to decide if she had enough courage to say what she wanted to say next. But she realized that the boy who stared back at her was not the same one that she'd thought she gotten to know so well over these past short weeks. He was a mean, callous stranger who deserved to hear every word that she had to say. Later, she wished that she had said it better, but she was glad that she'd said it all. "Well, it was a big deal to me. And you knew that, too. You knew I was a virgin. You did this just to be in FBI, didn't you? And then for you to be so nasty and pass my letter around and let that girl read it, much less read it all over the cafeteria. . . ."

"Hey, I didn't mean for Tricia to get it and read it to everybody. She snatched it when I wasn't looking."

"You know what, Ian, I can't stand you. I don't know why you're acting like this, why you're making this 180-

degree change, but you make me sick! Did you tell them you only slept with me on a dare?"

Ian shifted his feet and looked away from her without answering.

"Did you?" Kylie insisted angrily.

"Leave me alone, Kylie. It's over, let it die. It was no big deal."

"You are such a weak punk!"

"Not that weak, though. I was good enough for you, wasn't I?" he said, his eyes emotionless. "It's over, okay? I'm not trying to hurt you, but you're making it into something it wasn't."

For a moment Kylie's breath was caught in her throat as if Ian had kicked her in her gut. He looked away from her as she caught her breath again. When she continued her voice was quieter, but somehow more forceful. Ian felt the words like a convicted man's sentence. "Ian, I know that you really liked me. You go ahead and lie to your friends, and your new girlfriend, and even your punk-ass self. But you're not fooling me. I was there and I know how it was." The unshed tears in her eyes made Ian sparkle and particulate for a moment, as though she saw him through a kaleidoscope. She saw, just barely, the truth inside the boy who stood before her, lying. So she spoke some truth to him. "What happened between us was special for me, and for you. Even if you do stand there acting cold as hell, I'm not fooled. Maybe you have turned out to be this sick, mean person, but the earlier stuff was true, too. You're not *that* good an actor." She turned to go, but thought a moment and turned back to Ian. "And Ian, if you did sleep with me on a dare, I hope it was worth it. I really do."

"Whatever, Kylie. Just leave me alone."

"Believe me, you don't have to worry about that," she said as she walked away toward Dez and Tracy.

Chapter 19

Ian rejoined his crew after Kylie left. But everything they said and did just irritated him now. Nothing they laughed at was funny to him, nothing that they were planning to do interested him. All he wanted was to get away from them, be by himself, and think. He had truly messed things up and he had to figure out if and how he could fix things, and which ones, in fact, deserved fixing.

"I'm gone," Ian said to everybody and no one in particular.

"All right, man, check you later," Michael said.

"Call me, okay?" Tricia said.

"Okay," Ian answered.

"Yeah, later man," Dante said. When Ian got outside to

his car he sat in its cold interior as the motor warmed up. His and Kylie's words rang in his ears, again and again, loud and clear.

He had seen the hurt in her eyes when he'd said those things, and though he'd wanted badly to take them back, he couldn't make himself speak. When she'd said, "I know that you really liked me," he had wanted to tell her, "You're right, you're right."

At first he hadn't wanted Kylie because of how she looked: not stylish enough, not pretty enough. But somehow along the way things had changed, and he knew that he couldn't be with her because of what she drew from him, rather than asked of him. It was far more than he knew how to give. He was more real and more sincere with Kylie than he was with anyone besides his mother and sister. He hadn't been that way with a girl in so long that it felt a little like breathing new air. What she deserved, he realized, was someone she could count on, someone who, even if things fell apart, would still treat her like a friend. But he didn't want to be that someone, because the effort he'd have to make when things got tough was just way too hard.

And he wasn't prepared for tough. His father had taken the trouble to teach him that.

"Kylie, it's Tracy on the phone," Nae Nae called upstairs.

"Okay," Kylie said. "I got it," she said into the receiver when she'd picked it up. "Hey, Tracy."

"What's up, girl?"

"Nothing, you know."

"Have you spoken to Ian since you saw him at school?" Kylie had told her friends what had happened with her and Ian in the hallway. Dez wanted to get some of her cousins together to beat Ian's behind. Kylie had said not to talk crazy, none of that was necessary. Now at 6 P.M. Kylie had had a little time to let it all sink in. It was still hard to believe, but she was *beginning* to accept that the boy she loved was a deceitful, cruel person who could actually plot to use her so mercilessly while grinning in her face.

"No, I haven't spoken to him and I'm not expecting to. It's over. He made that plain. After how he's acted, it's definitely over for me."

"I know Dez's suggestion was completely crazy, but I do want to hurt him."

"Not me," Kylie said. "I don't want to get near enough to him to hurt him. I just feel so stupid."

"Don't, girl. You're not the first person to be played. Believe me, much worldlier people than you have been played royally. Ian's the one who should feel stupid. He should feel extremely stupid for dogging somebody as special and good as you. He's an idiot."

"I know," Kylie said sadly.

"Of course he is. You do really see that, don't you, Kylie?"

"I do. I just don't understand it, Tracy. All those things he said, the way he kissed me, the way he held me, I know that all of that wasn't fake. Some of it, probably a lot of it, was real. Not just for me, but for Ian, too. But he threw it all away.

"I don't understand how somebody could do that! I mean,

how could he do what he did with me on a dare, like me for real, and then trash me so completely? Can you tell me that? How is he so different from us?" Her voice was full of wonder and tears.

"I don't know, Kylie, I really don't. I wish that I had some sort of answer for you, something that makes sense."

"I know. The only one that can answer that is Ian, and I don't want to hear a thing he has to say."

"I hear that."

"Look, I'm going to get off the phone. I have some stuff to do around the house. I'll see you tomorrow at school."

"Okay," Tracy said. "See you later."

"Bye."

When Kylie got off the phone she did the few weekday chores that she had and started Nae Nae and Stevie on their homework. All the while her heart ached and she longed to be somewhere alone where she could crawl under the covers and cry. So she left her sister and brother working at the dinner table and went upstairs with her books.

She found that she could only concentrate for a few minutes at a time before her mind or heart was distracted by Ian. She wondered if he had laughed at her behind her back with his friends whenever he left her. She could hear him saying, "Aw, man, you should have seen how grateful that girl was for a kiss," or "I never had to pretend so hard to like a girl in my life, and the crazy thing is, man, she's falling for it!" She imagined Ian and his friends laughing and giving one another plays. Did he tell them how she smelled, or how her body felt? Did he mock her hair and clothes and the work that she did around the house, the time he spent with her little sister and brother, her quiet mother?

Now she understood why someone who'd paid her no attention before suddenly came out of the clear blue sky and not only asked for a dance, but a date, then another date, and another date after that. All so swiftly, too. He did it to win a dare, probably for that stupid FBI clique that he belonged to. Kylie knew about FBI, and she knew that its recruits had challenges that they must meet successfully. She just never connected any of that to Ian and her.

Congratulations, Ian, she thought, you were most definitely a success. By the end you had me fooled completely. Kylie lay her head down on her pillow and allowed the hot pressure behind her eyes and the pain that pushed against her chest to become the tears she had longed to cry.

An hour later the telephone woke her up. She had dozed off crying. "Hello," she said softly.

"Hello, may I speak to Kylie," a male voice said.

"Speaking."

"What's up, Kylie, it's me, Terrance."

"Hey, Terrance, what's up?"

"Nothing, I just called to talk, see how you were, that's all."

"Oh."

"How did that last quiz go?" he asked.

"Oh, it went well. I got an eighty-two percent. Thanks a lot, you know, your tutoring is excellent.

"It's no problem. I'm glad to help. Actually . . . I really like spending time with you."

"Thanks. Look, no offense, but I don't feel like talking right now."

"Oh," Terrance said.

"It's not you. I'm just . . . tired."

"Naw, it's no thing," he said. "You okay?"

"No, but I don't want to talk about it."

"All right," Terrance said. "Look, I just wanted to ask you something before we got off the phone—would you like to see a movie this weekend?" Terrance asked.

"Why? Do you have some sort of dare to complete?" Kylie snapped.

"What?" Terrance asked, confused.

"Nothing."

"No, what are you talking about?"

"Nothing. I can't go to the movies this weekend."

"All right. Is next weekend possible?"

"Look, Terrance, I don't think I'm going to be up to going to the movies anytime soon, okay?"

"What's with the attitude?" Terrance asked. He didn't sound angry, just interested.

"I might as well tell you, half the school probably knows by now. Do you remember that guy I introduced you to at my locker a little while back?"

"Yeah, Ian, right?"

"That's right. Well, it turns out he was only seeing me on a dare. Stupid me wrote him this letter and he took it and read it to all of his friends and let some girl read it to a bunch of people in the cafeteria. So, my attitude isn't with you, it's with Ian, and myself for being so trusting. I'm sorry I sounded snotty."

"No, that's all right. You're upset . . . and hurt. I understand."

"I guess that I'm just the kind of girl that can only get a date as a dare," Kylie said. She tried to sound light and sarcastic.

"Don't say that. Nobody's daring me. I'm just sorry that I've waited so long to ask you. I guess I let nerves get in the way. Plus, I could tell when he showed up at your locker that time that you were really into him."

"Poor judgment on my part."

"So you didn't walk around suspicious, thinking all guys were dogs. You shouldn't have to. We're not all like Ian."

If you only knew, Kylie thought. You don't even know that we had sex and he told everybody, she thought.

"I'm not like that, Kylie," Terrance said. His voice was kind and reassuring. She tried not to think of Ian, of how seductive his voice could be sometimes. But Terrance's voice wasn't seductive, it was . . . honest. Or at least she thought so, but what did she know? After all, she'd trusted Ian, too.

"Give me a chance. I know it's a little soon. But I won't hurt you like he did, I promise. We'll just go to a movie, get something to eat, and talk. I like you, Kylie."

"I don't know, Terrance. It's *real* soon, okay? All of this just happened today. I don't feel like doing anything right now. I wouldn't be any fun to be around. You've been real nice to me, I don't want to do you like that."

167

"All right, that's cool. But don't forget about me, okay?"

"Of course not. You're still going to be my math tutor, aren't you?"

"Yeah, bet."

"Cool." There was a pause again, and Kylie tried to think of a good way to get off the phone without seeming too eager to do so. "Well, I better get back to doing some homework, I'll talk to you later, Terrance."

"I'll see you tomorrow, right, in study hall for a tutoring session?"

"That's right, I'll see you tomorrow. And in class, too."

"Kylie?"

"Yes?"

"Will you call me if you change your mind about going out? We can do whatever you want to do, just give me a call."

"Thanks, Terrance. You really are sweet."

"But not too sweet, Kylie."

Kylie laughed for the first time that day since all of her troubles began. "I'll call you if I change my mind."

"Ian, I thought you'd never call. It's almost eleven o'clock, boy."

"Sorry, I got caught up with some homework," he lied to Tricia.

He'd actually spent the entire evening in his room, mostly in the dark, listening to other guys sing about women they'd lost. When Kim had knocked on his door a few hours into his pity-fest, he told her that he had a stomachache, and after checking to see if he needed anything, she'd left him alone.

What he wanted was to hear Kylie's voice in his ear, but he'd called Tricia, hoping that she'd at least be a pleasant distraction. But she wasn't.

"That's okay, I'm glad you called. Ian?"

"Yes?"

"I'm sorry that I did that with your letter."

"Forget it," he said shortly. Please, he thought, just forget it.

"Are you still thinking about her?" Tricia asked.

"No. That's over."

"Oh." Her word dropped into a silence Ian couldn't fill. He wished he'd never called her, wished he'd never said those things to Kylie, and wished that Kylie were lying beside him. Most of all, he wished he'd had the courage to be true to her.

"You don't want to talk?" Tricia asked.

"No . . . Yeah, sure I do. I'm just tired, that's all. What's up with you?" he asked. He listened as she chattered on. He knew that just a few weeks ago he would have been so glad to be listening to her. But now it felt like a job, and his quiet listening was a lie.

He was tired of pretending, he really was. But it seemed to him that sometimes the worst habits were the hardest to break.

Chapter 20

"Ian," Kim said in exasperation, "would you stop prowling around here like some sort of panther? Sit down someplace and keep still!" Kim had been noticing, or rather trying not to notice, her younger brother's restlessness for the last forty minutes. He couldn't seem to keep still for more than a few minutes at a time. They were seated in the living room watching old *Cosby* reruns on NickTV. Ian would get up and go to the window, sit for a bit, then wander into the kitchen, return empty-handed, and sit again. Then he was going up the stairs where she heard him moving about, then back on the love seat, then back up again to go into the kitchen. Kim had had about all she could take.

"What?" he asked distractedly.

"I said, keep your narrow behind still. You're moving too much."

"Oh." He looked around as though trying to figure out what he had been about to do. Television laughter filled the room.

"What's the matter with you, Ian?"

"Nothing."

"Okay," she said, unconvinced but knowing full well not to butt in. He was her little brother, and they were close, but Ian liked to keep some things private and she respected that. She was the same way.

"I don't know how to say it," Ian said.

Good, he wants to talk, she thought. It had been a long time since she had seen him so troubled that he couldn't keep still. A long time. And the last time was about their father letting Ian down again. "Just say it whichever way that it comes out."

Ian nodded at his sister and sat quietly for a few moments more. "I screwed up. With Kylie. I wrote her this letter telling her how much I liked her, and she wrote me back with a lot of personal stuff, and then I gave it to some of my boys to read. Then on top of that, this other girl snatched it while I was in the cafeteria, and read it out loud where a lot of people could hear."

"Damn, Ian."

"It gets worse." He took a deep breath and continued. "In the letter, she talked about losing her virginity with me."

"Oh, no."

"It gets worse."

Kim just shook her head waiting for the next small bomb to drop.

"Kylie found out and confronted me, and I acted like a complete jackass. So now she *really* hates me."

"Why, Ian? Why? Why did you act like that when you were the one who was wrong?" Ian's sister stared at him, mystified.

"I don't know. I really don't know. Stupid, I guess." Ian looked genuinely perplexed.

"Why did you give her *very* personal letter to a bunch of guys to read? What is the matter with you?"

"I don't know. I don't know!" He got up again and paced in front of the television, saw that he was getting nowhere, and sat down again.

"You should know something, Ian. I don't blame her for hating you." Kim looked at her brother, shaking her head, sensing that something wasn't quite right, but deciding not to press right now. Given how badly he had behaved, she was just glad that he'd opened up and talked. She didn't want to run him off. "What are you going to do now?"

"I couldn't even tell you. That's what I'm trying to figure out."

"You do like her, don't you? You seemed to be really into her."

"I did. I still do, a lot." He looked miserable.

"Well, you've got to get her back. Tell her how sorry you are, ask for another chance. Beg."

"I don't think I can. I think I've messed up too much for that."

"You have to try if you still like her that much. I just don't understand why you would do the things you did considering how you feel."

He just shook his head and glanced at the television. They had it good, he thought of the people on TV, in fourteen more minutes they'd have all of their problems neatly wrapped up.

"You're going to have to try, Ian."

"I don't think I can. She's not going to want to talk to me, and I'd only look like an idiot begging and pleading for her to give me another chance. I'm not gonna be a punk for anybody!"

"Oh, so you're thinking about your pride, huh? What about *her* pride?" his sister asked. "Did you ever stop to think about that?" They sat together quietly for a few minutes before Kim spoke again. "You are not Daddy, Ian. You may look just like him, but you are not him. You're better than he is."

Though she doubted that Ian would appreciate her actions, Kim was convinced that what she was about to do was the right thing. Her little brother was in pain and in trouble and, whether he knew it or not, he needed her help. She went through their telephone's caller ID. She recognized Kylie's number because it had been coming in over the last three weeks. She copied it down and dialed.

"Hello, may I speak to Kylie?"

"Who's calling?" a woman asked.

"Kim."

"Hold on a minute," Jillian said.

"Kylie," the woman called, "it's Kim on the telephone." Kylie picked up the phone.

"Hi, Kim," Kylie said. She sounded surprised.

"What's up, girl?"

"Nothing? What's up with you?"

"I was just talking to Ian. He's really upset."

"I doubt that."

"No, he really is. He told me what happened."

"He did?"

"Yeah. He feels really bad."

"Then why hasn't he called me to tell me? Did he ask you to call?"

"No . . . he doesn't know that I'm calling you," Kim admitted reluctantly.

"Oh. Well, that about says it all, doesn't it?"

"No, it really doesn't."

"What did he tell you?" Kylie asked. Kim told her everything that Ian had said, emphasizing how Ian was too ashamed to call her.

"I see he didn't tell you that he only had sex with me, was only seeing me, on a dare, huh?"

"What? Who told you that?"

"A friend. But when I asked Ian about it, he didn't deny it."

"No, he didn't tell me that."

"Yeah, well ask him about that." Both young ladies were quiet for a bit. "I guess you don't want me to help out at the shop on Saturdays anymore."

"Of course I do! You're not the fool, apparently my brother is. But I'll tell you, Kylie, he is truly messed up behind all of this. He really likes you."

"Not enough, Kim. Not enough."

Chapter 21

"So y'all gonna be sweet for the talent show?" Tricia asked Ian. She stood right in front of him as they waited in a long line for tickets to the new Will Smith movie. Ian was at the Star Southfield movie theater with Tricia, and other members of his crew and their dates. It was Saturday night, and the theater was packed, primarily with other teens, all well dressed, looking good, and scoping one another out.

"We'll be all right," Ian assured her, his voice cocky but light. He was having a good time with her. He really was, he told himself. Of course, it would be a great time if he wasn't thinking about Kylie every ten minutes. He kept wondering what she was doing, how she was doing, if she was over him, if she thought about him. He kept picturing her: the way she looked when they kissed that first time, the day she struggled to stay up on her skates, how good she'd looked after Kim had hooked up her hair, and the way he'd felt looking at her lying in his bed after they'd made love. He could hear her voice, smell her scent, and see her walk. He missed that girl so badly, way more than he had ever expected to.

"Is Ian Striver being modest?" Tricia teased. "You know, y'all are too sweet. Damn you can sing, boy!"

Ian grinned despite himself. "Thanks," he said. Tricia had stopped by the auditorium on Thursday and Friday to watch them rehearse. He'd spotted her sitting in the second row, center, with some of her girls. Afterward she'd met him out in the hall in the semiprivacy of a doorway for a kiss.

"This line is taking too damn long," Michael complained. Everyone agreed with him on that.

"I think I heard somebody up ahead say the computers are temporarily down," Christian volunteered.

"Great, I'm glad we got here early. They better hurry it up, though. I'm not going to the movies late, I wanna see the previews and everything," Michael complained.

"Well, when the line starts moving, why don't some of us go get the popcorn and stuff and the rest of us stay and get the tickets?" Michael's date, Janis, suggested.

"That's a good idea," Dante said. They spent some time organizing themselves, and most of them decided to be in the concession line group, with only Ian, Michael, Dante, and Tamar staying behind to get tickets. Money was exchanged, orders given, and the line moved a bit.

"So how are you and Tricia getting on?" Dante asked Ian.

"All right," Ian said, his tone unenthusiastic.

"'All right,' what do you mean, 'all right'? You sound like you're complainin', man!" Michael cut in.

"What are you talking about? Naw, I'm not complaining," Ian said.

"Well, you sound like it," Michael persisted. "'All right,'" Michael said mimicking Ian's tone and voice nearly perfectly.

"Shut up, man," Ian said chuckling, and Dante and Tamar joined in.

Michael laughed too. "You sound like you miss your little bony girlfriend. What was that dog's name, I never can keep it in my head." Ian forced a laugh.

"Shut up, Mike," Ian said as lightly as he could.

"Naw, hold up," Michael said as he warmed up to the subject. "Remember how she used to come creeping around our lockers trying to get your attention, lookin' all pathetic and needy? Damn, man, I don't know how you stood it for so long." Ian could feel anger boiling inside of him. Who the hell was Michael to talk about Kylie? He didn't know her. He wasn't good enough to wipe her shoes! "Did she bark when you screwed her, Ian? Come on, tell me, did the little doggie do a little barkie?" Michael fell all over himself laughing at his joke. Dante and Tamar joined in and Ian found that he just wanted to take his fist and smash it upside Michael's face.

"Shut up," Ian said, his voice serious, and heavy as death. "Shut the hell up, Mike."

"What did you say to me?" Michael stopped short.

"You heard me. Why do you always have to say

something nasty about her? Kylie, man, her name is Kylie. She's got a name and she's got feelings. And I want you to stop talking about her."

"What! Do you hear this fool?" Michael asked Dante as they all three moved forward with the line. "*You* gonna try to school *me* on how to act?"

"That was a messed-up challenge you gave me!" Ian shot back. "Messin' with somebody's emotions like that is screwed up!"

"You really *like* that girl, don't you?" Michael said in a softer voice. Ian said nothing, but he did not allow his eye contact with Michael to waiver. "Don't you?" When he saw that Ian wasn't going to answer, Michael continued, "Well, well, well." Michael looked from Ian to Dante and Tamar and back to Ian. "Look, man, don't call yourself going off on me 'cause you screwed up. If you didn't want to do the challenge you didn't have to. Nobody made you. You're feelin' all guilty now and you want to put it on somebody else, but don't even go there, Ian. Don't even go there. If you cared about her you should have stood by her and let all that other mess play itself out."

"Yeah, right! If I had stayed with her I would've gotten all kinds of flack from FBI, and you especially! You've had something smart to say about Kylie from day one," Ian countered.

"So did you, Ian! You didn't start out liking her, so don't try to put that mess off on me."

"Kylie's not FBI material, though, is she? She wouldn't fit in, would she?"

"Hell, you already knew that, man."

"So now what?" Ian asked, and his voice sounded like a threat.

Michael felt the eyes of his boys on him and heard the edge in Ian's voice, and he said what he felt he had to say, not necessarily what he wanted to say. "So now you need to make a decision: her or us."

"Is that right?" Ian glanced at Dante and Tamar, then looked Michael right in the eye. It should never have come to this, Ian thought just before he opened his mouth again. "Then I'm out."

"I never thought your ass was stupid, you let a girl turn you out like that? She ain't nothin', Ian! You could get girls ten times better hangin' with us, and you steppin' off for that? Stupid ass," he ended in disgust.

Ian turned to walk away and found Tricia coming toward him, laughing with her friend, pretty as a princess.

"Hey, Ian," she said, placing her hand on his chest, laughter still in her voice.

"Hey, Tricia, I'm sorry. I got to go. Can I drop you at home, or do you want to stay?" Ian asked.

Tricia looked at him more carefully. Ian looked as if he'd survived a train wreck. "What's the matter? Are you okay?"

"Naw, he's not okay. Are you, Ian? You gonna tell Tricia about your little plans?" Michael said.

Ian kept his back to Michael and his eyes on Tricia as he shook his head. "I just got to go, that's all."

"No, man, that's not all. Why don't you tell her what's really up?" Michael said.

"Yeah, right," Kylie teased her friend. "You could easily find ten guys willing to take you and Tracy out tonight!"

"And you, too," Desiree said. "You were already cute, Kylie, but Ian's sister really hooked your hair up. You look really good now. It shows off your face and those awesome eyes."

"Thanks, Dez," Kylie said.

"You're welcome, but it's only the truth." They reached their lockers and worked the combinations as they continued talking. "So if I hook up the dates, you'll go out with Terrance and try to get your mind off of Ian?"

"Yeah, sure."

"Are you still going to the Winter Talent Show?" Dez asked. She knew, just as Kylie knew, that while there would be fifteen acts in the two-hour show, FBI performers would be some of the highlighted acts. She knew that Kylie might not be up to seeing Ian under the spotlight so soon.

"Yes, I think so."

"It's not for another week, but tickets went on sale today and they're selling really fast."

"Is that right? I'll keep that in mind."

"Cool," Dez said. "Where is Tracy?" she asked, looking around.

"I don't know, but here comes Terrance," Kylie said. They both watched Terrance approach from down the hall.

"What's up?" he greeted them as he neared.

"What's up, Terrance?" Kylie said. "This is one of my best friends, Desiree Hessup—Dez, Terrance Wells." The two said hello.

"So, you headed home?" Terrance asked Kylie.

"In a little bit, we're waiting for our girl, Tracy Lane." Terrance nodded. "So . . . I changed my mind, Terrance."

"You did?"

"Yeah," Kylie said.

"I helped," Dez interrupted. "I told her to get out and smell the roses."

"Thanks," Terrance said with a smile in Desiree's direction. "So when would you like to go? What would you like to do?"

"What about going to play laser tag this Saturday? I thought a group of us could go, Dez, Tracy, and a couple of guys that they might bring," Kylie suggested, suddenly getting an idea. "We could get pizza and then go play for a while, or vice versa."

"That sounds good," Terrance said.

"Cool. I'll give you a call and we can work out the details," Kylie told him.

"Bet."

Kylie could see the warmth in his eyes and she liked it. Although she wasn't sure how much she liked him romantically, she knew that she liked him as a friend. But all the while that she had been talking to Dez, Kylie had been making minute checks in the hallways for Ian. And that hadn't stopped once Terrance came by. She wished she could stop looking for him, she was starting to get on her own nerves. Then again, it had only been seven long, agonizing days since their break-up. That wasn't long enough to stop looking for someone you still cared about so much.

Kylie bit her lip and made herself concentrate on the very attractive and kind boy standing in front of her. "Tonight, okay? I'll call you tonight."

"Okay," Terrance said with a smile.

As he walked away Desiree tilted her head slightly to the side for a better look. "That boy's got a really cute butt."

"Dez!"

"What? He does." Desiree smiled at Kylie. "Really cute." Kylie laughed, tilted her head to the side as she watched Terrance walk away, and said, "You're right."

When Tracy came they updated her on their plans, and Tracy said that everything sounded cool. She and Dez talked about which boys they might consider asking as the three left the building together and headed out to Desiree's car.

They drove along quietly for a bit as they looked out at the snow-covered city. "Home," Kylie said.

"All right, I'll call you," Dez said.

"Me, too," Tracy said.

"Me, too," Kylie said, and they all laughed.

"She seems better," Tracy said. They watched Kylie's back retreat as she went through the door.

"Yeah, some."

"It takes a while to get over someone . . . even if he is a complete jerk," Tracy said sadly.

Chapter 22

"'Hold on to the love, hold on to the dream, don't let it go away, do all you can to make it stay, baby. Hold on to the love, hold on to the dream, don't let it slip away, give it all to make it stay, baby,'" Ian sang the words with a quiet richness that reverberated in the nearly empty auditorium during the dress rehearsal for the winter talent contest. Everyone stood still as he finished his last note and Marcus's fingers tripped lightly over the last few notes on the keyboard: effortless, poignant, and perfect. Then one of Ian's competitors reluctantly began to clap and the rest of the kids who were gathered around for the last rehearsal joined in the applause.

"Sweet, man," a guy said.

"Thanks," Ian said as he met his hand for a play. Ian was

rehearsing solo today, because that's how he'd be performing. Since the falling out at the theater Ian couldn't *pay* FBI members to sing backup for him. He didn't want them, anyway. As he climbed down the stairs and let the next act take over the stage, there was more praise from some people he knew. Ian barely took it in. He was trippin' on the irony that the song he was set to perform tomorrow afternoon was precisely how he felt about his situation with Kylie. When he'd picked the song two months ago it was because it was a rising R & B hit by a popular recording star. The words meant very little, but girls screamed at cute boys who sang ballads well, and all of that would help him be a star in the show and a star at school. That was all he had cared about . . . two months ago. *Now* what he thought was that the song was about Kylie and him and what they'd lost because he had been so stupid and selfish.

When he got out of rehearsal it was six o'clock on a Thursday evening, a week after he had destroyed his relationship with Kylie. He warmed up his car in the parking lot and gave Marcus a ride home. He'd never been over Marcus's house, but as he followed the directions Ian realized that Marcus lived near Kylie. Once he'd dropped him off he sat in his car tapping the steering wheel for a few moments, then shifted the car into drive and headed for Kylie's. He hadn't seen her or spoken to her in eight days. He was too ashamed. But, now, he had the impulse to see her and to apologize, and he wouldn't resist it as he had several times already, he would follow it.

When he pulled into the parking lot he saw her mother's

car parked, took a deep breath, and pulled in beside the Accord. Before he lost too much of his nerve he got out of the car and walked to the door. His hand paused only a moment or two before he rang the doorbell.

"Ian," Jillian said. "We haven't seen you in a while," she added pleasantly after opening the door. "Come on in." She sounded so welcoming that Ian knew that Jillian had no idea how much he had hurt her daughter, or even that he had hurt her at all.

"Thank you, Ms. Winship," he said as he stepped inside.

"Kylie's not here, though," Jillian said as they stood in the tiny foyer.

"Oh." He couldn't keep the disappointment out of his voice.

"She's just around the corner, at the library with Stevie and Renee."

"Oh."

"Why don't you go on around?" Jillian suggested.

"Okay. Thanks, Ms. Winship. I'll see you later."

"All right." Then he stepped out of the door back into the darkening day.

He walked around the corner to the library, making tracks that immediately blended in with those already marking the day-old snow. He tried to think of what he would say to this girl that he had disrespected and hurt so badly. Nothing seemed good enough. He didn't feel capable of saying what she deserved to hear. He knew what he should say to her. He should say, "Kylie, I am so sorry, sorry beyond any words that I know to say. But if you'll let me, I will work to show you just how sorry I am. I think about you all the time and if you would have me, I want you to be my lady. Please forgive me, girl. Give me another chance." And then, if she were still listening, if she hadn't walked away or closed herself off to him in such a way that he could read it in her eyes, then he would take the back of his hand and brush it against the softness of her brown cheek and kiss her warm lips tenderly. He took in a deep breath of winter air and let it out loudly, closing his eyes for a moment. And when he opened them Stevie was running toward him with his arms flung out wide and his jacket only halfway zipped up.

"Ian!" Stevie shouted.

"Stevie, my man," Ian called in returned and when the little boy reached him Ian stooped and gave Stevie the hug he expected. When Ian rose he saw that Nae Nae stood near, and that Kylie had stopped, several paces away.

"What's up?" Nae Nae greeted.

"What's up, girl? You been hittin' the books with your big sis?"

"Yeah. I got an A on my homework," Nae Nae said.

"That's good, Nae Nae." Then he looked at Kylie who was staring at him with those black eyes that he couldn't read right now. "Do me a favor and go hang out with Stevie over there for a second while I talk to your sister."

"No problem," Nae Nae said.

Ian walked over to Kylie and stood in front of her, just staring and trying to get himself started. He was glad to see her again, even if he couldn't say a word. Kylie looked right back at him for a while, and then sighed in exasperation and started to walk around him. That woke him up and Ian took a step to block her path. "I'm sorry, Kylie."

"Leave me alone, Ian," Kylie said without looking at him.

"I can't."

"Don't kid yourself. You can, and you did, and you will again."

"Kylie," Ian said as he still blocked her path. "Kylie, I *am* sorry." She looked at him then. "I know I never should have done you that way."

"Whatever, Ian." She considered him silently for a few moments. "But you *did* do me that way, didn't you? And it's done now, and so is all the damage you did. Do you have any idea how damn humiliating it is to walk the halls with *everybody* knowing the exact time and way I lost my virginity? Can you imagine what it's like walking around *knowing* that you're the stupidest girl at a school like Cross? Of course you don't. 'Cause you're just the young mack daddy that got yet another girl to give it up, right? You're the player and I'm the one who got played." A tear fell from her eye and he wanted to wipe it away and pull her close to him, but he was afraid to touch her. She stared at him until he was forced to lower his eyes. "I gotta go."

"Kylie, please, can't you give me another chance?"

"Are you kidding?" she asked, and her face was suddenly so full of fury that Ian took a step back. "Can you really be serious?" she asked, and there was space between each word, space enough for him to feel the weight of her anger. This time when she stepped to walk around him he did not block her path. He stayed where he was, facing away from her, not even responding when Nae Nae and Stevie called good-bye.

"All right now," the emcee shouted into the microphone, "we know why ya here! We know what ya want! And we're prepared to give it to yaaaaaaaa!" The packed auditorium of 2,500 teenagers exploded in applause and raucous cheers as teachers patrolled the aisles. The winter talent show was off the chain again: loud, exciting, thumpin', and stylin'. The first eleven acts had been really good, but everyone knew that the best acts were yet to come. There was a gospel group that could make even this rowdy crowd yell "Amen"; a girl dance group that was athletic, sexy, and sharp, FBI's dance group, Ian's solo, and FBI's main rival dance group. Kylie, Desiree, Tracy, and several other kids who they hung with around school had seats in the fourth row, center. Kylie had to admit that despite her nervous anticipation of seeing Ian perform she had been enjoying the show. It was well done, the groups were well rehearsed, and while the audience was rowdy, it wasn't mean or out of control.

The gospel group was wonderful; a soulful mix of harmony, solos, emotion, and rhythm. The girl group that followed them was inventive and clever, sinfully rhythmic and coordinated. The crowd roared for both groups. But when FBI's music began to pulse loudly through the auditorium and the stage went completely black, the crowd leaped to their feet and cheered. Mist began to roll up from the foot of the stage and a dimmed searchlight began a slow prowl among the performers. Then there were creeping figures making their way across the stage, and the cheering reached a fever pitch for one of the most popular groups in the school. The FBI tore the house down with their routine, which told a story through dance of a young man rising from the ashes of violence around him. Their CD was a compilation of segments from three popular dance cuts and a couple of R & B songs that kept the audience hopping and rocking. Their steps were intricate, sharp, and graceful with a careless sexiness to them that was irresistible. The crowd roared for quite a while after FBI's dance group left the stage and the curtains closed.

Then they reopened, and the audience found the stage entirely dark once again. When the first soft notes of the romantic ballad began to stir, Ian's voice rang out from the darkness, deep and resonate. He said, "This one is dedicated to the girl with the midnight eyes. I'm sorry, baby." Kylie's heart skipped three beats and, about two dozen girls from various places in the auditorium let out screams.

"Kylie, is he talking about you?" Tracy shouted in order to be heard over the crowd.

"Yes, yes!" Kylie shouted back; she had never dreamed that Ian would have the nerve to send her a sign so publicly. Dez and Tracy squeezed her arm and clapped as the routine started. It went beautifully. Ian carried the solo like a professional, and Marcus Shipp's fingers *owned* that keyboard. Ian wore blue jeans, an oversized red T-shirt, and a sultry expression. Kylie would have only been more proud of Ian if he were hers, honestly and rightfully.

Unbelievable, Kylie kept thinking. She felt like she

could live in this moment forever where Ian sang to her, and only her, in front of hundreds of people and while so many girls screamed like they wanted him to be theirs. *She* knew what it was like to kiss him under a dark sky on a cold winter night in front of the Detroit River. *She* knew what is was like to have him hold her up as she floundered on ice skates, his laughter mingling with hers as they went round and round. *She* knew what it was like to fall in love with him, and make love with him.

And then the song ended.

Ian sang the last note, long and true, with the microphone held in one hand and the other arm fully outstretched, his eyes closed, his expression earnest. It was a wonderful pose of drama and supplication, manliness and romance. It was a great ending to a great performance . . . except the excitement wasn't quite over. Out of the left wing of the stage one of Tricia's friends strode, with her long, slender brown legs stretching beneath a tight red minidress, her hair swinging, and catching the light with its shine. She walked until she stood before him, then she pressed herself against him, and placed her hands behind his neck before she drew his head down to hers for a kiss. The crowd's hoots and whistles rang out as they watched the spectacle.

Very few people know what it's like to step, mistakenly, entirely by surprise, into a black hole. The hole swallows you up before you really even get a chance to realize the horrible place that you have fallen into. It is frightening, overwhelming, and swift, swifter than anything you can imagine. It swallows sound and heartbeats, logic and reason, and that was where Kylie found herself. The only way that she could see to get out, without shouting out or crying in public, was to turn and run. She had to get out of the auditorium as quickly as she possibly could.

Ian felt as though he was walking in a dream. Things were unreal, out of joint, moving in slow motion, and happening just out of his grasp and control. He had been singing to Kylie, that's all. He couldn't see her, he wasn't even sure that she had come, but he hoped so, and he sang each note envisioning her face, her eyes, and the feel of her in his arms. In the song, on stage, he was calling her back to him, apologizing to her, and caressing her. He filled each note with his longing for her and he prayed that she heard. When the girl, Diamond, came onto the stage he did not hear her over the crowd's cheers, or notice her, because she wasn't part of the act. By the time she stood before him and pulled him down for the kiss, he still had not gotten his bearings. He hadn't wanted it, hadn't expected it, and he ended it as fast as he could without tossing Diamond onto the floor. But he knew that it was probably too late. If Kylie were there, the damage would have been done. All that she would have seen was that he had sung this incredibly romantic song and then kissed some other girl. Period.

As soon as the curtains closed, Ian moved to rush off the stage. He mumbled his thanks to congratulations handed his way. If he could, he wanted to get out into the hallway and see if he could find Kylie. If he knew her even a little, he figured that she would have left the auditorium after that kiss. The hallway formed a rectangle around the auditorium. He

he could memorize in order to make himself a better person, a better man. He had come to realize, after all that had happened and after several in-depth discussions with Kim, that that was the root of his problem. He was selfish, and self-absorbed, and willing to hurt and discard a good person, a really good person, for his own personal gain. He wanted to talk to Mr. Hill about it, but he didn't want him to know how badly he'd behaved.

He made himself think about the fact that Kylie spent her days helping to raise her brother and sister, and he only had to take care of himself. While she was preparing dinner for Renee and Stevie, helping them with their homework, and keeping them out of trouble, he was procrastinating about his homework and griping about washing the dishes. He worried that he was too lazy to ever be a better person. He thought about talking to a man about his problems, and was sad to think that he'd rather go to Mr. Hill than his own father.

But at the same time he knew that Kylie was worth it. She was worth the effort it took to be a better person and a better man. He even considered the possibility that he was worth the effort as well.

He just wasn't sure of the formula to get him there.

At the Winter Talent Show, Kylie knew that Terrance was seated at the end of the row behind her. She just didn't want to think about it. There he was, kind, honest, cute, and available, and she was still drooling over Ian. Last weekend they had all gone out for laser tag, but she still missed Ian so badly that she could taste it.

When Ian humiliated her yet again by kissing another girl in front of the entire school, Kylie could only think to flee. She'd brushed past Terrance as she went, but by then she had completely forgotten about him. She did not know that he had nudged Tracy and asked for Kylie's jacket. She didn't know that he had then pushed through the crowd and followed her up the aisle, her coat in hand. When she'd gotten out into the hall she had planned to leave the building, and wait outside until her friends joined her. It was only then that she realized that she'd left her coat back in the auditorium, and she knew that she wouldn't be going back there to get it any time soon. "Damn," she'd said and then Terrance was beside her in the foyer of the building asking, "Are you all right?" He'd had such genuine concern in his tone and eyes that she'd answered honestly "No." After she had waved Ian away, Terrance put her jacket around her shoulders and held it as she put her arms into it, and then he'd walked with her friends and her to Dez's car. When he'd asked if he could call her that night, she'd said yes. The fact that he had gotten up, brought her coat to her, and stayed with her a while, meant something to her. He was exactly the kind of boyfriend she wished Ian had turned out to be.

As Desiree drove them home it was very quiet, with Desiree and Tracy making only the occasional comment. They were kind enough not to bring up the horrible subject of the talent show and Ian's behavior, and Kylie was thoughtful enough to ignore their idle conversation. That was the luxury of having good friends.

At home, Kylie had picked up her sister and brother from up the block, given them a snack, and started dinner. She tossed a simple green salad and cleaned and seasoned some perch, then put the fish in a plastic container to keep until her mother came home. Then she sat herself down to get some homework done, because even if her love life was headed down the toilet, she had an essay due on Monday that she'd already put off for two weeks. All she had to show for those two weeks was a few notes, a very sketchy outline, and a nearly completed novella. She had fifteen pages left to read in Edith Wharton's *Ethan Frome*. Kylie opened up her spiral to the *Ethan Frome* notes she'd taken during her teacher's lecture, reviewed them quickly, turned to a blank page on which to take notes, and cracked the short book open. At least it had *that* going for it.

In an hour's time Kylie had finished the last fifteen pages of the book, and taken down some notes that she thought might be helpful for her essay on "Seizing the Moment" in the novel. She worked on an outline and a start for the essay for another hour. Writing was not her strong suit, and she had a real problem in that she couldn't get rolling on an essay until she had a beginning that was acceptable to her. It usually took her a while to get that beginning and this essay had been no exception. Stevie had moved on to playing with his action figures upstairs in his room after the first half hour of work, and Renee lay on the living room floor coloring quietly. Two hours into her effort, with only a few stops to check on Stevie and Nae Nae, Kylie was ready to put her homework away for a while.

Her mother came home shortly after that, and after hanging up her coat, kissing all three children, and washing her hands she got right to frying up the perch. Jillian had Stevie and Nae Nae pick up their things, wash their hands, and set the table. Afterward they all sat down to a hot dinner and a talk about their day. Kylie didn't bother them with the biggest event of hers; what was the point? Instead, she was grateful for the activities that had filled up the time since she'd gotten home. She had tried to give each one her undivided attention so that Ian and her troubles with him were pressed to the back of her mind. Sitting at the table, listening to her family laughing and talking made her feel a little better.

The telephone rang, and seconds later Nae Nae called Kylie to the phone.

"Hello?" Kylie said.

"What's up?"

"Oh, hey, Terrance. What's up?"

"I was just calling to see how you were doing."

"I'm all right. Can you hold on for a second?"

"Sure."

Kylie spoke to her mother, "Can I talk now, and do the dishes later?"

"Yeah, go 'head. I'll get the dishes tonight."

"Thanks, Ma." Then she turned her attention back to the phone. "So what's going on with you?"

"Not much. Practice, work, school."

"You play first base, right?" Kylie walked down to the basement as she talked.

"That's right."

200

"I hear you're pretty good."

"Well, I practice hard. My game is coming along."

"Mmmm. I see," Kylie said. "That's not quite what I heard."

"What did you hear?" Terrance asked.

"I heard all-city *and* varsity since ninth grade," Kylie said with a smile. He was easy to talk to.

"That right?" She could hear the smile in his voice. "You've been checking up on me, huh?"

"Yeah, a little. I'd think that you would be telling anyone you just met how good you were."

"Naw. My pops says that boasting is a sign of a poor upbringing."

"You're cool with your father?"

"Sure. I mean sometimes we have our differences, but on the whole, yeah, he's straight."

"He lives with you?"

"Yeah. My parents have been married for twenty years."

"Oh, for real? Dang, that's good."

"What about you? Do you and your father get along?" Terrance asked.

"I hardly know him, he hardly knows me. I only see him every once in a while."

"Oh."

"Yeah." Kylie decided to change the subject. "So, I guess I don't have to ask if you're ready for that algebra quiz."

"No, you don't have to ask. I'm ready. But I'll tell you something else I'm ready for."

"What's that?" Kylie said.

"Another date with you."

Kylie paused for a moment, hoping that she'd find the right words. She wanted to be as honest as possible without being hurtful. "I like you, Terrance, but . . ."

"Definitely not a sentence any guy wants to hear the end of," Terrance said in a half-joking tone.

"I know, but I want to be honest with you. I like you. I really do. But the truth is, I'm not over Ian, yet, and I don't want to play you. Not even a little bit. Not that I think I have it like that," Kylie added hurriedly. "But I don't want to give you the idea that things are one way, when they're really another."

"That's fair enough." He paused as if deciding what to say next. "But for me, Kylie, you definitely do have it like that."

Kylie felt like kissing him. Not because she was any more over Ian than she had been five minutes ago, but because Terrance had just said something that made her feel so good about herself, and that made her feel pretty good about him. She needed to hear that, especially now. She wished, a little, that she had hooked up with Terrance *before* she'd hooked up with Ian. Things could have been so different for her if she had. But she only wished it a little. Despite the pain Ian had caused her, there was no denying the magic he had brought into her life. She'd get over the hurt eventually. It didn't seem like it now, but she would, she knew that. The magic that she felt with Ian wasn't worth letting him dog her, she had sense enough to realize that. But maybe she could savor the memories of it later, she thought.

"Thank you, Terrance."

"It's just the truth, that's all."

"Maybe we could start with something a little more low-key than a date."

"Like what?" he asked with interest.

"Like just sittin' back talkin' someplace."

"Sounds cool. Any ideas?"

"Not really, not right now."

"You like to play video games?"

"Yeah, actually. Some," Kylie said.

"Well, you should come over here. We could play games, talk, chill. It would be straight. And my moms or pops would be here so you wouldn't have to worry about me trying to climb all over you," he joked lightly.

But Kylie found it a little difficult to laugh since that's exactly what Ian did almost every time that she'd been to his house. Not that she'd fought it. Just the opposite, she'd enjoyed it. Still, that is what they did whenever they got together. But, she reasoned with new clarity, if it was Ian's goal to have sex with her as quickly as possible in order to win a bet, then he would be sure that they messed around hot and heavy whenever he could maneuver it.

"Kylie? You still there?" Terrance asked. She hadn't realized that with all her thinking she had left Terrance hanging.

"Yes, Terrance. I'm still here. That would be nice."

"Oh yeah?" Terrance said. His voice was thick with playful flirting.

"Not the climbing all over me, silly!" Kylie said with a chuckle. "The video games. That might be cool."

"All right. You just let me know, okay? No pressure."

They talked for a little while longer with a light pleasantness that relaxed Kylie. Terrance was smart and funny and he took his education seriously. He had confidence without being cocky. She was flattered that he took an interest in her, and she marveled at the irony that four weeks earlier she would have been thoroughly charmed with the idea of a boy like him to hang out with. But now that she'd been struck by the Ian virus it had spoiled her appetite for healthier fare. She shook her head in wonder as she forced herself to find the thread of Terrance's words because her mind had wandered again.

That conversation with Terrance had been Friday night. And now, three days after the talent show, on a snowy Monday she sat in history class unaware that right then Ian sat in Algebra III trying to figure out a way to get her back.

Kylie had made up her mind over the weekend to make a 3.0 grade-point average her future, and her passion for Ian, history.

The high-rise condominium that Ian's father lived in had spacious apartments about three hundred feet from the Detroit River. Their seventh-floor residence had a view of a landscaped running path that lay beside an expanse of what spring would turn into a green lawn that stretched toward the river's beach. Now the lawn was covered with a layer of snow and the running path was neatly shoveled into a ribbon of cement. Ian had just laid his baby sister down for a nap after

---~♥~---

"I wondered when you'd get back down here," Mr. Hill said when Ian came into his office on Monday. "You out of class or is this your lunch hour?"

"Lunch hour. What's up, Mr. Hill?"

"Same ole' same ole', trying to save the world one child at a time." His smile was nearly a laugh.

"Sounds like a cool job."

"It is. You won't hear me complaining. So what's up with you?"

"I wanted to ask you something."

"Ask away."

"How can you be a good man? I mean, to a woman?"

Mr. Hill smiled, then tented his fingertips and placed them against his lips. Ian knew that Mr. Hill had been married for sixteen years. One time he had seen Mr. Hill standing outside of a car with his wife and they were the only ones in the school parking lot. Classes were in, and Ian was looking out of the window when he should have been looking for a book on the classroom bookshelf, and he'd noticed the couple. While Ian watched they kissed and they kissed like two people in love. Ian had never told Mr. Hill what he'd seen, he felt it would be an invasion of his privacy. But he thought that maybe Mr. Hill knew how to keep a woman happy if he could stay married for sixteen years and still have her kiss him like that.

"That's not an easy question," Mr. Hill said.

"I know."

207

"I'm still working at it myself." He paused for a moment, then spoke again. "At the same time, there are some basic things that you can do to give yourself a fighting chance, so to speak."

"Okay."

"Be honest with her. Admit when you're wrong. That one might take a little while, but you still gotta do it. Listen to her, even when you don't really want to. Let her know how much you care about her. If you don't, somebody else probably will. And be willing to change for the better. Of course, that one isn't always easy to see, but the woman will usually be happy to help you see where you're wrong." He laughed then. "Needless to say I don't always follow my own advice. But I'm getting better, little by little."

Ian nodded.

"Everything's a process," Mr. Hill said. "Can I ask who she is?"

"Her name's Kylie."

"Good luck."

"Thanks."

Chapter 24

Kylie's second day of work was two Saturdays after she and Ian broke up. Kim picked Kylie up early, and they got to the salon before anyone else. Kim put the radio on and they moved around the shop getting ready for the day's work. After a while Kim stopped refilling bottles of shampoo and conditioner and watched Kylie line up different-sized combs and curling irons before she said, "Can I ask you something, Kylie?"

"Sure," Kylie said as she lay another curling iron out.

"I'll understand if you don't answer."

"Okay," Kylie said, and she gave Kim her undivided attention.

"Why did you do it with Ian so quickly? I mean, especially if you were a virgin."

Kylie wore a small, sad smile when she answered. "Mostly he was really good to me, you know? I had never had a boy pay me so much attention and treat me so well."

Kim shook her head in despair and disgust. "I love Ian, he's my brother, . . . but damn, he can do some messed-up stuff sometimes!"

"You know," Kylie began quietly, "I had a bad feeling about Ian a few times while we were talking." Kim looked at her closely waiting for her to continue. "I don't know, something in my gut told me to be careful, but I didn't listen. Ian had never paid me a bit of attention, and all of a sudden he couldn't wait to call me and take me out again and again. All of a sudden he was inviting me over his house. I know that I'm not like any of the other girls he's usually with. They're always pretty, well-dressed, perfect hair. Still . . . I wanted to believe that he really liked me. But if I had had any sense I . . ."

"What?" Kim urged.

"If I had had any sense I wouldn't have ignored the fact that he didn't want me around his friends."

"Damn."

"I know. And I was a virgin. I let my first time be with a boy who was only trying to get into some stupid club!" Kylie was barely able to get the words out before tears surprised her. Kim reached over and stroked Kylie's back gently.

"It's okay," Kim murmured several times. When Kylie had gotten a handle on her tears, Kim said, "Let's go and get something to eat. We still have forty minutes before my first client."

After they'd ordered, and the food had arrived Kim brought the conversation back to Ian. "Kylie, don't get me wrong, the bad guy here is Ian, no doubt. But you need to promise yourself something."

"Never trust boys again? All men are animals?" she asked wryly.

"No, because that's not true."

"I know," Kylie said thinking of Terrance.

"You should promise yourself never to ignore your gut feeling again. Listening to yourself will protect you again and again and again. Don't try to explain away how you feel in order to fit what you might *want* at the moment. 'Cause your gut is telling you what you *need*, and that's more important."

Kylie allowed Kim's words to sink in for a few quiet moments, and then she said, "I promise."

"Yeah, but I didn't say promise me, I said promise yourself, that's where it counts the most." Kylie smiled at her new friend and silently promised herself. "Now, I'm going to say this, not to hurt your feelings, but because I care about you."

"All right," Kylie said with a feeling of apprehension.

"Next time you have to think a lot more of yourself than to let some boy who won't even speak to you in front of his friends have something as precious as your sex, and even more precious, your heart." Kylie just stared at Kim, swallowing and trying not to cry. Not because Kim's words were mean or harsh, but because they were true. "I know Ian. He's cute, he's charming, he's smart. But he also thinks that he's a player. He's more concerned about being popular than he is with getting good grades. I'm still trippin' that he actually did this to you. I have to admit, I'm ashamed of him right now, but not totally surprised, not really. And you're worth more than giving someone like that your virginity."

"How can you say things like that about your brother to someone who isn't even family?"

"They're true," Kim said with a shrug, "and I like you and want to help you." Kim drank some orange juice. "Don't get me wrong, though. I love my brother, I'd give a kidney if he needed it, and he already has my heart, so I think I can afford to tell someone like you a little of the big, bad truth about him. Besides, I'm not telling you anything you don't already know."

Unfortunately, Kylie thought, Kim was absolutely right.

"Kylie, will you give Shavonne a bottle of water?" Kim asked. This was Kylie's third Saturday at the beauty shop and she found that she liked the job. She shampooed hair, conditioned it, and put the client under the dryer. Then, if the client desired, she gave them an ice-cold bottle of water. Kim kept her own little stash in a small fridge and additional packs were stored in her trunk. The twenty-five-degree day kept those plenty cold. With Kylie's assistance and judicious scheduling, Kim was able to keep her clients moving in and out of the salon at a reasonable pace. This kept her clients very happy, because they saw that Kim, unlike too many other beauticians, valued their time and their business. The bottle of water was a nice touch.

Kylie was alternately humored and scandalized by the things she heard the clients confide to Kim. They seldom whispered, not seeming to mind that Kylie could easily hear. Kim had continued to behave as a new, warm friend. She and Kylie laughed and chatted during Kylie's short workday and she always gave Kylie twenty-five dollars on top of doing her hair for free.

With only fifteen minutes left in her shift, Kylie found herself laughing out loud as Denise, a thirty-eight-year-old client, related the story of having to tell a handsome, financially secure almost-boyfriend that his breath smelled too bad for the relationship to go further if he didn't deal with the problem, when the front door opened and the bell signaled the arrival of a customer. Kylie looked over at the door without any real interest, and saw Ian stroll into the shop. The sight of him wiped the smile from her face, and for an instant, froze her to the spot. It had been over two weeks since their breakup and she hadn't seen him in seven days. Seven days of avoiding him in the hallways, of missing him, of despising him. She had even told herself that she had begun to get over him, at least a little bit. Seeing him again now, unexpectedly, she could only recall what it was like to kiss him.

She reminded herself that she had to keep her feelings in check at all times when he was around. She did still care for him, she was certainly still attracted to him, and though her instincts had told her something was wrong with Ian's attraction to her, they had also told her that something was very, very right. She knew that in the conflict was the danger. He looked at Kylie as though she were the only one in the shop. He came over to where she stood while she tried to make herself busy straightening up the bottles of shampoo, conditioner, and hot-oil treatments that lined a nearby shelf.

"Hi, Kylie," he said softly. She could have kicked herself for the way her heart reacted to his voice, but she didn't say anything.

"Are you gonna just ignore me? That's all right," he said to her softly. The quality of his voice reminded her of how he spoke when they were alone, kissing and holding one another. "But I know you get off in a few minutes, and I'll be waiting for you. I need to talk to you. I was hoping you'd let me give you a ride home." Kylie moved on to straightening the already neat piles of tan-colored towels.

"What's up, Ian?" Kim called.

"What's up, Kim?" he answered.

"Who is that?" a bold young lady asked Kim, in a stage whisper.

"My younger brother, Ian."

"How young?" the twentysomething client asked.

"Too young for you, girl," Kim said.

"I'll be outside, okay?" Ian said to Kylie.

She did look at him then, and though she had intended to continue her silence the tender look in his eyes prevented her. "All right."

When her shift was over she went to say bye to Kim, who ushered Kylie into the back room. "So what are you going to do?" Kim asked.

214

"He wants to give me a ride home and talk. I'm going to let him. That's all."

"All right. Always keep in mind what your value is, though, and don't compromise that."

"I hear you."

"Here," Kim said as she gave Kylie her pay for the week. "You're a really good help to me."

"Thank you," Kylie said. "I'll call you, okay?"

"All right. See you."

The last few days had been sunny and in the upper thirties. The little snow that had been on the ground had melted away, and though it was still a cold forty-two degrees, it was sunny again with a beautifully blue sky. Ian stood outside the shop in his shearling coat, holding a small bag.

"Hi," he said when she came and stood in front of him.

"Hi." They just looked at one another for a few silent seconds. It seemed like so much longer to both of them.

"I got us some juice," he said with a nod toward the bag in his hand.

"Thanks."

"Are you ready to go?"

"Yes." They walked to his car and he walked around to open the door for her. Kylie noticed the effort. "Thank you," she said when he had gotten into the car and shut the door behind himself.

"You're welcome, Kylie." He started the engine and drove in the direction of her home, some fifteen minutes away. After a few minutes he asked, "Can we stop somewhere to talk?"

"All right."

He drove to a small playground nearby and parked in its lot. There was a brief stretch of brownish grass, defeated by the winter season, and a forlorn-looking swing set, slide, and playscape. It all etched a lonely picture against the blue sky. Ian parked the car but left the motor running so that the car would remain heated. He handed Kylie a strawberry-kiwi juice and a straw and took the same out for himself. She thanked him and they drank quietly for a while.

"Kylie," Ian said into the quiet, "can you try to give me another chance?"

"I don't trust you, Ian. It's that simple."

Ian shook his head, as though trying to clear his thoughts. "I know, and I know what I'm about to say is going to sound like a line, but I've changed, Kylie, I really have." She just looked at him with those eyes whose black seemed to go on forever. "And if you give me another chance, you'll see, believe me."

"What about the talent show? Did you think I just forgot about that?"

"I didn't have anything to do with that. That guy Michael is still pissed that I quit FBI's initiation, so . . ."

"You quit FBI?" she asked, surprised.

"Yeah. So he told Tricia to go out on stage and do that, but she wouldn't, so he got her friend to do it. There's nobody else but you."

There was no denying the earnest note in his voice. Half of her wanted to believe him, but the other half told her to hold back and not trust him. "Maybe, Ian, maybe. But the problem is, the one taking all the risk is me . . . again. The person with the most to lose is me . . . again. Bottom line, all I have is your word, and you're the same person who dogged me in the first place."

Ian tapped the steering wheel with one hand. "You're right," he said slowly. "Still the only way that you can know that I've changed is to give me another chance. If you do, I promise, you won't be sorry." Kylie shook her head silently. Ian flicked on the car stereo system and rap music played softly. "So are you seeing that guy on the baseball team?" He'd told himself not to ask, but he really wanted to know.

"His name is Terrance."

Ian looked directly at her, "Are you seeing Terrance?"

"No, not exactly."

"But he wants to, huh?"

"Yeah. Not that it's any of your business, but we talk on the phone and we have hung out."

"Oh," he said. If Terrance were there now Ian was sure that he would punch him in the face. Not just because Terrance was trying to squeeze up on Kylie, but because Ian feared that Terrance would treat Kylie much better than he had when they were together. "Is he part of why you won't give me another chance?"

"No! I already told you why." Her voice held an edge of anger to it. "Don't you think that would be enough by itself?"

"Yeah," he admitted.

"I'm ready to go home now," Kylie said. "Ian," then she paused, "the letter you wrote me, was it just part of the scam?"

"No," he answered. She stared hard at him. "Yes and no.

I meant what I said in the letter . . . and I . . . needed you to write me back, as proof of how you felt." He felt as though the words were being torn out of him. He wanted to lie and deny it, but at the same time he really was trying to change. Still, it was painful as hell to admit how shamefully he had behaved.

Without a word Ian put the cap back on his juice, moved the car into gear, and started driving her home. All during the drive his mind churned with possible ways to persuade her. But none seemed right and he was running out of road. He wasn't going to beg, but he needed to let her know how very much she meant to him now. He couldn't find the words in time, and her place was just a couple of minutes up the road now. He got her home, parked the car, took off his seat belt, and turned toward her.

"I know how badly I acted, Kylie." He was talking to the side of her head. "Come on, look at me, girl. Please." She turned to him reluctantly. "I didn't start talking to you because I liked you. I did it to meet a challenge for FBI. But I ended up liking you . . . so much." He looked away for a moment and said in a near whisper, "I'm ashamed of how I treated you." When he looked back at her he could see what she had been guarding ever since he walked into the beauty salon: how much she still liked him was written all over her face. The sight flooded him with warm emotion. He hadn't truly known if she still cared for him at all, or if he had killed all of her feelings for him. He leaned toward her and placed a gentle kiss on her closed lips, and when she did not resist he began to French-kiss her, and his heart stirred more when he felt her mouth moving sweetly under his. He moved his hand to cup the side of her face, and for the first time in nearly two weeks he felt real hope. And then she pulled away.

"Talking to you didn't make things better for me," she said. He could hear in her voice and see on her face that she was fighting back tears. "This has just made it all harder. I don't trust you, Ian! Get it?" She made her way out of the car and slammed the door behind her. He watched as she hurried to her front door, unlocked it, and looked at him for a moment before shutting the door behind her.

Chapter 25

On Christmas Eve Ian knew that Kylie was working at the shop with Kim. He delivered a small box wrapped in shimmering red paper to her house and left it in the care of Kylie's mother. Inside was a small crystal prism that fit into the palm of her hand. It was pyramid-shaped, skillfully proportioned, and sat atop an onyx stand the color of her eyes. When struck by light, a perfect spectrum of color could be seen through the prism, each color keenly vivid and appealing. It was beautiful. That evening Kylie called him.

"Hello, Ian."

"What's up, Kylie?"

"You know that I can't keep it," she said getting right to the point.

"Well then, throw it away, or give it away, because I won't take it back. I bought it for you."

Her next words were spoken gently, "I can't throw it away or give it away."

Ian felt his heart expand with the words. "Then keep it," he answered just as gently.

"Thank you, then," she said. "Merry Christmas. Bye, Ian."

"Merry Christmas, Kylie."

Ian found it amazing that feelings for another person could fill up so much space in his heart. He awoke each morning with thoughts of her, he had thoughts of her off and on all day, and ended each of his days with Kylie on his mind. He often found himself thinking about what they'd do if they were together: places they'd go, things they'd talk about. He missed the way that she listened to him, and the way that she shared her thoughts so honestly. The Christmas break and all of January passed that way. It made the days and nights too long.

He hung out with some of his friends from ninth and tenth grade and stayed off his mama's nerves. He spent time with Kim, got a job at a deli, tried a little harder at school, and thought of Kylie. His life was full and good, but the sensation of missing her made it all seem somehow less.

He saw her sometimes in the hall at school, and in a way those times were worse than when he didn't see her at all. Sometimes she was alone, at other times she was with her friends or with Terrance. He wondered what things were like with Terrance and Kylie. Were they becoming closer? He felt sad at the thought. If he and Kylie were near enough they said no more than "hi," and he felt compelled to behave noncha-lantly, as though seeing her didn't faze him at all, since that's how she acted toward him.

But when February came with Valentine's Day approach-ing, he was no more over her than he had been in early December. And he didn't want to be over her. And then he got what he thought, what he hoped, was a very good idea.

During their time apart a new semester began and Kylie's grades were good in all of her classes. And why not? She had discovered that one of the best ways to take her mind off Ian was to delve into her books. She wasn't making any quan-tum leaps, but she saw definite improvement. In math, English, and history she had actually moved up a full grade. In Spanish, computer programming, and chemistry her grades had moved up several percentage points.

She hung out with Tracy and Desiree, spent time with her brother and sister, read books, hung out with Terrance, studied, worked at the salon with Kim, and sometimes hung out with her. She'd stopped calling Ian and Kim's because she didn't want to give Ian the impression that she was still try-ing to get in touch with him. If she wanted to talk to Kim she just called her cell phone.

But she missed him every day. She missed his calls, and after weeks apart she still had to resist calling him sometimes. She missed their laughter mingling together over some story that he told her. She missed kissing him and touching him and staring into those golden eyes. All of this longing embar-

rassed her because he had made a fool of her. The very
his calculating, and then acting in order to humilia
stung the most vulnerable part of her heart, roused her
and shamed her, all at the same time.

She had taken the crystal prism that he had given h
Christmas and placed it on her dresser where, during pa
the day, it caught the sunlight. She loved it. It reminde
of how Ian could make her feel when she had been falli
love with him. The colors shot out onto her wall, and s
mered on her brown arm when she put it in the light's pa

In the beginning, the days crept by, then there v
weeks behind her, and now nearly two months. Febru
swept onto the stage with a heavy snowstorm that shut do
school for two days with ten inches of snow in sixteen ho
Impulsively, Tracy, Desiree, Kylie, Renee, Stevie, and a f
other kids decided to meet at a park not far from their hon
and have a snowball fight. The day and the snow were perfe
for it. The air was cold and crisp and the sky a grayish-blu
and empty of clouds. There was very little traffic on the roa
because of the snow and the relative quiet made it seem a
if the day belonged to only them. Even the snow had tha
perfect balance of wetness and fluffiness to form the bes
snowballs.

They split into teams and dashed across the slightly hilly
terrain, hid behind trees, tumbled, screamed, and laughed.
They finished by making snow angels, all the big kids imagining, for a little while, a time when they were small like
Stevie and Renee; and Renee and Stevie were glad to be
included in the big kids' outing. Kylie lay in the snow,

looking up at the sky, a quiet dome above her, the snow nearly a cocoon, and imagined Ian kissing her again.

When they were too tired and wet to go on, they went over Tracy's house and had hot cocoa and chips and cookies, listened to music, acted silly, and talked. Afterward Kylie, Terrance, Stevie, and Renee walked and talked for several blocks together before Terrance caught the bus home. When he was gone they continued walking. Stevie and Renee told stories of things that had happened at school, and Kylie listened and advised when necessary.

But neither that day, nor the ones that slipped by after it kept away the thoughts of Ian. With the middle of February approaching she found, to her dismay, that she was no less in love with him now than when he'd last kissed her.

Cross had a Valentine's Day tradition. Students bought sing-o-grams, balloons decorated with hearts and words of romance, and carnations for their Valentines for delivery during class second through seventh hours.

Terrance met Kylie at her locker just before first hour and gave her a small box of chocolates. Kylie gave him a heart-shaped box of chocolates. Second hour a sing-o-gram arrived for a very pretty girl named Carla early in the hour, and in the middle of the hour Mitchell Simpson received one from his girlfriend. Just before the bell rang a young man arrived carrying three huge balloons. One read "Happy Valentine's Day," another "I'm Sweet on You," and the other was decorated with pink and silver hearts on a red backdrop.

"May I deliver this to . . ." He paused to check his notes. "Kylie Winship?" he asked the teacher.

"Sure," the teacher said with a smile and went back to checking papers. Kylie's head snapped up in surprise. Terrance had already given her the chocolates. This would be too much, considering that she wasn't interested in going with him and had told him so. The young man walked over to Kylie with a smile and placed the balloons' strings in her hand. "Happy Valentine's Day," he said in front of the whole class, "from Ian Striver."

Third hour Kylie got a delivery of six pink carnations. "Ian Striver says, 'you're always on my mind,'" said the young lady who delivered the flowers.

Fourth hour she received six red carnations. "Be my Valentine," the young man said, "from Ian Striver."

Fifth hour a young man approached her in the cafeteria and sang the first two verses and the chorus of the very same ballad that Ian sang at the talent show. He finished with, "Happy Valentine's Day, from Ian." When he finished all of the girls at their table except Desiree called out "Aaaww!"

Sixth hour Ian gifted her with six white carnations and the message, "I hope it's been a beautiful day, Ian."

Though she tried not to be at first, Kylie was impressed. She was carrying a bouquet of eighteen large carnations, three huge balloons floated above her head, and she couldn't help humming the tune of the love song. It was all over the school that he had showered her with gifts and attention today. Kylie was almost scared to see what would happen seventh hour. What more could there be?

Seventh hour another boy showed up and delivered a card sheathed in a deep pink envelope. "Ian Striver says

'Happy Valentine's Day, Kylie,'" the young man said with a grin. Kylie thanked him, and when everyone finished teasing her and went back to work, she opened the card. There was a picture of two beautiful children of about five years old, a little boy and a little girl, dressed in the old-fashioned attire of the 1920s. He was sharply suited and she wore a lovely dress. They both had the same brown skin as Kylie. The girl carried a small bouquet of red roses, and the boy leaned in to kiss her on the cheek. Kylie opened the card and saw the only printed words on the right-hand flap: Happy Valentine's Day. On the left hand flap Ian had written her a brief note.

Dear Kylie,

I guess you get the message, I want you to be my Valentine. But I respect the fact that you might not be ready for that yet. I know all of these gifts don't mean that you can trust me. Only time will show you that. So I am willing to wait. That's what I've been doing, that's what I'm going to do.

Happy Valentine's Day. You deserve it.

Ian

It was a happy Valentine's Day. The best that she'd ever had. And Ian had given it to her. But he was right, she did still need time, because something inside of her was telling her to wait. By the end of the day even Desiree grudgingly admitted that Kylie might, possibly, at least accept Ian's apology. And though she didn't know quite why she needed to wait, she would take Kim's advice and listen to her instincts.

Kylie remembered the end of the conversation that she and Kim had had about listening to your instincts at the restaurant. "My mama taught me to listen to my gut, that voice from deep inside myself," Kim had said.

"Did she teach Ian that, too?" Kylie had asked.

"Yes."

"Do you think he listened?"

"No." Kim flipped a sugar packet over. "Yes." Kylie stretched her hand out flat on the tabletop between them. The sunlight that came through the wide window had warmed the space. Kim flipped the packet again. "Maybe."

"Ian," Kim said outside of his bedroom door.

"Come in."

"Look," she handed him an envelope with both of their names on it. He recognized the handwriting as that of his father.

"What's this?"

"See for yourself."

Ian opened the envelope and pulled out a folded sheet of paper. He unfolded the sheet of paper, and two plane tickets fell out. They were dated for April 12th, the first day of spring break, and they were destined for Orlando, Florida. *See you then*, his father had written on the sheet of paper.

"I'll be damned!" Ian said.

Chapter 26

"Now the beauty of poetry," Ms. Embry said, "is that it has the ability to encapsulate our feelings and thoughts into clear, sometimes concise language. Thus, at times when we analyze poetry for meaning we must endeavor to expand the information, if you will, to gain a richer understanding of the meaning locked inside the lines of the poems," she finished with a smile. "In some cases we must make sure that we are clear on the vocabulary that the poet is using, or we may miss even more of the meaning available in the poem." Ian sat listening to Ms. Embry's preface to the poetry lesson in English class, but his mind was partly elsewhere.

It was two weeks after Valentine's Day and he had not heard from Kylie. Three days after Valentine's Day he had finally asked Kim what Kylie's reaction to his gifts and words had been.

"She made me promise not to tell you," Kim said as she washed dishes.

"But you have to tell me, Kim, I'm your brother!"

"Yes, and she's my friend, and you dogged her, so I don't have much pity for you."

"Kim, please, I'm dying here," he said.

"Well . . ." Kim said thoughtfully, "I suppose that if you happened to guess it, I could acknowledge if you got it right."

Ian smiled his thanks. "She hated it?" Kim shook her head no. "She liked it?" Kim shook her head no. "She loved it?" Kim nodded her head yes once. Ian hollered, "Yes!"

"That's not all, though," Kim said. "And I really shouldn't be telling you this."

"Too late now, tell me," Ian urged.

"It made her cry."

He had been so hopeful that she would call him or speak with him at school that the evenings and days following Valentine's Day were filled with keen anticipation. But when the fifth day passed, and he still hadn't heard from her, he knew that she was not going to call him. She wasn't just waiting for the right time, which is what he'd told himself during the first few days. She was not going to call him.

"So let's take out last night's homework and use it to begin today's lesson," Ms. Embry said. Those words called Ian back to the lesson at hand. "Last night," Ms. Embry continued, "you were to read the assigned poem and look up the words 'trite,' 'emboldened,' 'opulence,' 'optical,' 'scarlet,' and 'empyrean.' After looking the words up and recording their definitions, you were to read the poem again. How many of you found you were better able to appreciate the meaning in the poem after looking up the words?" Nearly everyone's hand, including Ian's, went up. The teacher smiled, "Good. Let's share the definitions aloud, read the poem, and talk about it." She pointed to the words "opulence," and "optical," on the board. "What do 'opulence' and 'optical' mean, Candace?"

"'Opulence' means characterized by an abundance," Candace called out.

"Break that down into laymen's terms, further," the teacher invited.

"It means having a lot of something; and 'optical' means having to do with sight," Candace said.

"Good. Ian, do 'scarlet' and 'empyrean.'"

"Scarlet is red, a bright red, and the empyrean is a high point in heaven," Ian said.

"That's right. Alexia, what do 'trite' and 'emboldened' mean?" Ms. Embry asked.

"'Trite' is when you use something so much that it's boring, like if a boy uses the same lines to try to get a girl's attention, then his lines become boring or trite." The class laughed. "Embolden is to make bold or to give courage."

"Very good, Alexia." She looked around the room. "Now, Marvin, read the poem aloud to the class, then I'll read it, and finally, I'll give you a little time to read it silently, then we'll talk about it."

Marvin began to read the poem in his clear, melodic voice:

"Red swept across the sky in an opulence of optical
splendor
That took my breath away
And I realized then
With the certainty of scarlet against snow
That I loved you.
I wanted to tell you then,
Right away,
Underneath the sycamore tree where we kissed
And I touched the empyrean
Swiftly and gently
But everything I thought of sounded trite.
Anyway, I know that you are gone
Dashed away on that last flight to New Orleans,
And I am, as always,
Emboldened too late."

Last night, when he'd done his homework, Ian had thought the poem was cool. But he'd had a lot of work to get done, so he'd copied the definitions from the dictionary, read the poem, and moved on to his history work. But as Ms. Embry read it again in class, and changed the rhythm of her voice and the places where she put the emphasis on words and phrases, she helped to bring about a better understanding of the poem for him, and by the time he read the poem to himself silently, he understood it completely. Because it was as simple as this: he loved Kylie like this speaker loved the person in the poem. And it was as clear as day, or "scarlet against snow." He didn't just like her very much, he loved her.

And though the thought exhilarated him, it also scared him. For he hoped that he had not been, like the lover in the poem, "emboldened too late."

He delivered the letter to her house in an envelope that same evening. Ian gave it to Nae Nae when she answered the door, and then he left without ever crossing the threshold or seeing Kylie. The letter's contents were simple. He had copied the poem, with the definitions to the words they'd covered in class. Then he wrote:

> Please read this poem. We had to study it in English class, and it says how I feel about you. I love you, Kylie.
> Ian

Chapter 27

With the Saturday sunlight dancing through the crystal prism in her hand's palm Kylie saw each color in all its distinctive beauty. She knew, now, what had been holding her back.

She read the poem and the letter again, for the fourth time, and sat as she had each time, very still and quiet. She was listening for what her gut had to say. She'd had to read the letter four times to be sure of what she heard, because she had to listen beyond the singing of her heart.

So she was quiet. And still. And patient.

She loved Ian and she had needed to know that he loved her. Because if he did, if he could admit that he did, then he would be taking just as great a risk as she was. Things would be all right, she thought. They would be much better, much sweeter, than all right. And so she made her decision.

She picked up the phone and dialed.

"Hello, Ian?" she said. "It's me . . . Kylie."

Acknowledgments

Well, God is good, and I would not have another opportunity to publish without God's grace! But there are so many others to thank, and if you're truly blessed, and I am, there are too many to thank individually. I'm only thanking a few folks by name, but my heartfelt, bursting-over, can't-you-see-me-grinning-and-tearing-up thankfulness goes out to EVERY SINGLE PERSON who has extended their support to my writing career! That's right, that includes you. And I'm not being glib either, I mean that "thank-you." I started trying to thank folks individually and I was well on my way to writing another book, plus I had that horrible sinking feeling that I was missing some people who were very important. So I stopped that, and wrote this.

Thank you so much to my incredible husband and friend, Omar; my two beautiful children, Aaliya and Omar II; my mother, Mae McKeithen; my grandmothers Pauline Embry and Mary Washington; my cousin Marsha Robinson and very young aunt Shelly White, who read all my stuff; aunts Sandra Johnson, Tammy Sassy, Catherine (Cat) McKissic, and Esther Robinson; and my uncles Chris Embry and Willie Whitley. Also, thanks so much for your support and love: Geraldine Davidson, Ahmad Karim, and Ruby Karim, my in-laws. Thank you to everyone who read *Played* during its development, especially my students at Cass Tech High, including Ashley Beverly, SherAaron Hurt, Elisse Ramey, and Mariah, class of '04. Thank you to all the students of Cass Tech High School, the school that Cross High is based on, for buying *Jason and Kyra*, talking it up, and urging me to get this next one out. I want to thank my wonderful friends and colleagues Yolanda Cargile, Rakia Johnson, Ebony Thomas, Shar Willis, Pam English, Monica Jones, and Marcia Barbie who read and edited early versions of *Played*. Thank you also to outstanding authors Jacqueline Woodson, Sharon Flake, and Sharon Draper for their encouragement and advice. To Vicki Green, my great friend and fellow writing group member, thanks for reading *Played* over and over.

To all of the people who gave *Jason and Kyra* a try, thank you for all of your encouragement and support! I appreciate you spreading the word about that book, and hopefully, this one.

I greatly appreciate every librarian and bookseller around the country who pushed *Jason and Kyra*! Special thanks goes out to librarians in the Detroit Public Libraries, Baltimore area public libraries, and Chicago Public Libraries, and booksellers in the Detroit area.

Thank you to my wonderful agent Janell Walden Agyeman at the Marie Brown Agency. I love the way you just keep making things happen for me!

Finally, I am indebted to all of the fabulous folks at Hyperion Books for Children who believed in this little engine that could: my wise and clever editor Alessandra Balzer, my dedicated, astute, and funny assistant editor Arianne Lewin, as well as charming Angus Killick, Margaret Cardillo, Scottie Bowditch, Dana Torres, Elizabeth H. Clark, and RasShahn Johnson-Baker, as well anyone else at HBFC who made the wheels go around so that *Played* could hit the shelves.